# The Doctor

Center Point
Large Print

**This Large Print Book carries the
Seal of Approval of N.A.V.H.**
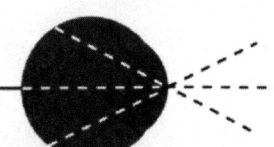

**WEST OF THE BIG RIVER**

# The Doctor

*A Novel Based on the Life of Dr. George Goodfellow*

**CLAY MORE**

CENTER POINT LARGE PRINT
THORNDIKE, MAINE

This Center Point Large Print edition
is published in the year 2021 by arrangement with
Western Fictioneers.

Copyright © 2014 by Clay More.

All rights reserved.

The text of this Large Print edition is unabridged.
In other aspects, this book may vary
from the original edition.
Printed in the United States of America
on permanent paper.
Set in 16-point Times New Roman type.

ISBN: 978-1-63808-085-5

The Library of Congress has cataloged this record
under Library of Congress Control Number: 2021940854

# Chapter 1
# THE OATH

*Tombstone, Arizona Territory, 1891*

Dr. George Goodfellow removed his stethoscope from the man's bare back and went back to his roll-top desk.

"You can get dressed now, Stanley," he said as he picked up his pen and made some notes on the record card in front of him. "You have a slight bronchial irritation, but nothing too serious. I'll make up a cough linctus for you and drop it off at your office before lunch."

Stanley C. Bagg, the five-foot tall owner and editor of the *Tombstone Prospector* and laterally, also the owner of the *Tombstone Epitaph*, tucked his shirt into his pants and pulled on his jacket. Then he pulled out a pair of wire-framed spectacles from his breast pocket and settled them on his thin nose.

"Thank you, George," he said, standing and immediately provoking a coughing fit. He covered his mouth with his hand and then thumped the front of his chest, which seemed to have the desired effect in stopping the cough. "I guess it is inhaling all that darned paper dust and ink fumes that does it."

The two men were old friends, as were their wives and daughters. Or at least, their wives had been good friends until the month before when Dr. Goodfellow's wife Katherine died in Oakland from the tuberculosis that had plagued her for years. And both men were known to be forthright in their opinions and in their manners. Stanley was a bullish, combative newspaperman who for all his lack of height was a formidable man to cross. He had been prepared to serve a jail sentence for contempt of court when he refused to pay a fine imposed upon him by District Judge Barnes. Fortunately, several of his friends, including his friend and doctor had donated money to keep the newspaperman out of jail, while leaving his personal integrity intact.

As for Dr. George Emory Goodfellow, he had built the premier medical practice in Tombstone and garnered a considerable reputation throughout the Southwest as the surgeon to have operating on you, if you had a choice. He was prepared to push back the frontiers of his craft and perform operations that no one had tried before or even thought to be possible.

"It is probably more to do with those evil-smelling cigars that you insist on smoking. I've told you before, you are poisoning your system."

Stanley guffawed. "And that is coming from a

man who was advising me that a good pipe keeps a lot of diseases away when we were chatting just last week."

George stood up. He was taller than the newspaperman. He was thirty-six years old and powerfully built, like the boxing champion he had been at the United States Naval Academy at Annapolis in his youth. He had been hotheaded back then and gotten involved in a fight at the Academy, the result being a win for George. Unfortunately, his prize was expulsion and discharge for lack of respect for discipline. That had been the time when he had chosen to make his career in medicine.

He had black hair with a central parting, a full mustache and steely eyes that could smolder with anger, twinkle with amusement or which could be reassuring in the extreme. As usual he was wearing a bow tie and a dark suit with his polished knee high boots.

He pointed to the wall above his desk upon which hung his framed medical degree beside a framed copy of the Hippocratic Oath, and in a small glass-fronted box a silver double-headed eagle medallion of Austria, which had once been the property of Emperor Maximilian of Mexico. Stanley had written an article about it when it had been presented to Doctor George Goodfellow by President Porfirio Diaz, along with a horse named El Rosillo in 1888 following the Sonora earthquake. They were given as tokens of Mexican esteem after he had loaded up his wagon with medical supplies and led a party ninety miles to Bavispe, Sonora, Mexico to treat survivors and injured. Then in the following months he had returned along with Camillus Sidney Fly, the town photographer, to study and record the effects of the earthquake. Together they travelled over seven hundred miles through the Sierra Madre Mountains. Both Camillus Fly's photographs and George Goodfellow's maps and reports earned national praise. The photographs of the earthquake rupture scarp were widely syndicated and George's geological study had been praised by the United States Geological Service.

Stanley knew that his friend was proud of the award, yet he was far prouder of the fact that the townsfolk of Bavispe had called him *El Santo Doctor*, the sainted doctor. His fluency in Spanish had helped, since he could communicate, explain and reassure the injured in their own tongue. It was typical of the man that he cared more about what his patients thought of him as a doctor than he did for all the accolades and prestige that he seemed to accumulate with little effort. He was just a natural subject for newspaper coverage, one of those characters that the frontier seemed to throw up every now and then.

But it was to the framed oath that George

directed his attention. "See that Hippocratic Oath, Stanley?" he asked rhetorically. "You know as well as I do that I live by it, as best I can. If I take someone on as a patient I'll give him or her the best treatment I can and advise them to the best of my ability. You have to accept that sometimes, like when we were chatting last week, my best may be impaired. If you recall we were playing poker at the time in the Crystal Palace Saloon and we had both drunk four or five whiskies. I actually said that a good pipe kept some diseases away, on account of pipe tobacco's natural ability to keep pesky flies and bluebottles away from the vicinity. And as you well know, the good Lord blessed us here in Tombstone with more than our fair share of the creatures."

His hands went up to grasp the lapels of his coat, a slightly pompous mannerism of his that many folks found intimidating. Mostly because it was usually accompanied by a slight raising of his jaw and a triumphant twinkle in his eye that signaled, at least in his mind, that he had either won, or was about to win an argument.

"So, my friend, you can see that the advice I gave you was the best I could give under the circumstances."

Stanley opened his mouth to protest when there was a sudden commotion from the waiting room outside. Voices were raised and there were exclamations of amazement. Then there was the noise of heavy boots racing across the wood floor and a beating on the door was followed by it being immediately thrown open.

"Doc Goodfellow! You've got to come over to Campbell and Hatch's Saloon and Billiard Parlor. There's a guy dying there."

George recognized the messenger as Walt Harper, one of the ushers from the Schieffelin Hall. He could see the panic in his face.

"I didn't hear any shooting. What is it, a knifing?"

"It's Red Douglas. He's choking and seems to be having some kind of fit."

The doctor had already sprung into action. He had grabbed his black bag and dashed to a cupboard from which he took out a couple of small wooden cases and threw them into the bag.

"Stanley, don't you come. That cough will start up if you try to run. Get going, Walt, I'm right behind you."

"And miss a story?" Stanley rejoined him. "Not on your life. I'll just take the stairs nice and easy and I'll meet you there."

But the town doctor had already gone. As he charged through the waiting room he barked a quick, "Emergency call, folks. I should be back in half an hour."

Then he was out the door and dashing down the outer steps of the Crystal Palace Saloon from his office.

As was often the case when folks saw Dr. Goodfellow racing someplace he attracted a number of followers who tagged on behind him. Tombstone was that sort of place. It had a lot of folks who seemed to have an unhealthy interest in sudden death. As long as it wasn't their own.

It took a matter of moments for George and his unwanted entourage to dash around the corner onto Allen Street and enter Campbell and Hatch's Saloon and Billiard Parlor.

Dr. George Goodfellow had set up his shingle on the second floor of the Crystal Palace Saloon in 1882, when the saloon had been built by Frederick Wehrfritz after the old Golden Eagle Brewery had burned down in the second of two Tombstone fires. The first fire a year earlier had been started when someone dropped a cigar on a barrel of whiskey in the Arcade Saloon. It burned down several other buildings on Allen Street, including the original Campbell and Hatch Saloon and over sixty other businesses.

There was a crowd gathered by one of the pool tables. At the doctor's entrance shouts went up and the crowd parted to reveal a man writhing on the floor, clawing at his throat, his heavy-bearded face almost purple and his eyes rolled upwards so that most of the whites of his eyes were showing. He was convulsing, his boots beating out a macabre tattoo on the floor.

"Give me room!" George cried, shoving a couple of onlookers roughly aside.

He knelt by the man and quickly assessed the situation. The man's mouth was open and lodged inside was what at first sight appeared to be a green apple. But as George put a finger on it, it became clear that it was a green clay ball from a 15 ball pool set.

"We couldn't get it out, Doc," someone said.

"Yeah, he threw a couple of us off when we tried to help him," volunteered another.

"The damned fool had won and was doing his usual showing off trick. He put that whole ball in his mouth."

"Only he couldn't get it out for some reason," another said, stating the obvious.

"His breathing is obstructed," Dr. Goodfellow announced. "How long has he been having a fit like this?"

"Three, maybe four minutes."

The doctor straightened to his feet. He pointed to the nearest four men. "You and you take an arm each and you two each take a leg. Hoist him up on this table."

With a sweep of his arms he sent balls from an abandoned game to the side wall of the table.

"Where's Bob Hatch?" he asked as the convulsing man was manhandled onto the table.

"He's at the post office. You want me to fetch him?" Walt Harper said.

"No," George replied as he opened his bag and drew out the two wooden cases he had brought with him. "I just wanted to warn him that I'm about to mess one of his tables. There will be blood."

He opened the first case and took out a scalpel. "Get me whiskey," he snapped.

One of the bartenders promptly threw a bottle to one of the crowd and it was uncorked and presented to the doctor.

"Is it to steady your nerves, Doc?" someone asked.

"No, you darned fool," George replied dryly. "It's to clean the blade." With which, he poured the liquor over the scalpel blade.

"Are you gonna cut his jaw muscles, Doc?" another asked in horror.

"Nope!" George replied, as he squinted at the blade. "You four men, hold his arms and legs real firm. And you other two, hold his chest. I'm about to cut his damned throat."

# Chapter 2
## GHOST TOWN

Stanley C. Bagg had arrived and as befitted his prominence as the newspaperman par excellence in town, he was permitted a passage through the crowd to witness the impromptu operation being carried out by Dr. Goodfellow atop the pool table.

The four men that Goodfellow had commandeered to assist him had their work cut out, for the bearded patient was bucking on the pool table. George himself had climbed up on the table and had one knee on the man's chest while he felt the man's throat with his left hand.

"In case any of you are interested, or think I've gone plumb loco," the surgeon boomed out, "I'm feeling just under his Adam's apple. There's another cartilage below it called the cricoid cartilage and a gap between the two covered by the cricothyroid membrane."

He grunted with satisfaction. "Here it is! Now you men hold him tight. If I don't get this done in the next few seconds we've got a dead man on the table."

Stanley looked on in wonder at the way George

Goodfellow took command of a situation. He was also aware that George appreciated it when folks understood the drama of surgery, for so often when he was called to operate, there was a life hanging in the balance. Almost mechanically, Stanley whisked out his notebook and a stub of pencil and began making notes.

Steadying the patient's throat as best he could with his left hand George made a firm incision between the area he was holding and spreading apart with his index finger and thumb.

Blood spurted upwards hitting him in the face. He ignored it as he widened the gap and a whooshing noise indicated that he had made a hole in the trachea.

"Done it! I've given him an airway."

With his right hand he opened the other wooden box he had brought with him from his office in preparation. From it he took out a curved silver tube that had a flattened disc surrounding the top aperture. He immediately inserted it into the incision in the man's throat and then, producing a silk suture and needles he dexterously stitched it in place.

The patient's color quickly turned from purple to a healthy pink and he stopped convulsing.

"Now he's just unconscious," George announced, as if the clientele of the pool room were medical students watching a surgeon at work. "If anyone doesn't like the sound of bones breaking, I suggest you clear out or cover your ears up now."

"Lord Almighty, Doc, what you gonna do to the poor guy now?"

"Apart from saving the damned fool's life, you mean?" George asked without looking at the questioner. "Actually, I'm just going to stretch his jaw a mite so I can get this ball out of his mouth. The temperomandibular joint only likes being stretched so far and there's a good chance I'm going to break his jaw."

And indeed, several strong men in the audience winced, as there was a noise not unlike the cracking of a turkey wishbone.

Stanley C. Bagg was not one of those who looked away. He watched Dr. Goodfellow perform the procedure then scoop the pool ball out of the patient's mouth before nonchalantly rolling it backwards the length of the pool table to land in the pocket with a resounding thud.

He noted that down. It would finish his article off very well.

Later, after admitting the patient to the Cochise County Hospital, George returned to see the half dozen patients who had dutifully and patiently waited to consult him. Three of them had bad coughs, but none had any signs of inflammation on their chests, so he gave each of them a small bottle of demulcent of his own invention. Joe Nokes, a miner, had an inflamed thumb, for which

George applied a small poultice of magnesium sulfate to draw out the pus. Mrs. Fiona Parker, the librarian who was also an assistant teacher at the school, had a mild case of conjunctivitis for which he prescribed a Borax eyewash, and Harold Marsh, one of the bartenders at the One-eyed King Saloon, complained of abdominal pain, which George was sure was caused by the gradually swelling liver that was the result of Marsh's daily intake of a bottle of whiskey. George gave him a lecture on excessive drinking before sending him off with some powdered dandelion root to help detoxify his liver and settle his pain.

Once he had seen Harold out, George went on his daily round of home visits. Although he did his best to encourage patients to visit his office during his appointed consulting hours, there were still a good number of cases that he decided to visit at home. The miners' cabins south of Toughnut Street were regular places to visit to check on the progress of miners with broken legs, crushed feet and hands. And of course there were always babies to be delivered in all parts of town and new mothers who had to be watched to ensure they didn't hemorrhage or get puerperal fever, or some other complication that could see their young one orphaned.

Thank the Lord that science was giving doctors a helping hand, he thought as he completed his examination of a newborn baby and then trimmed the umbilical cord stump.

There had been too many mothers who had died from infections and too many babies who had died in the past, after uneducated folk had cut their umbilical cords with anything sharp at hand, like a sickle or a knife that had been used for cutting meat or scraping mud off boots. It had been ignorance that had killed all of those babes and young mothers. Not just ignorance on the part of ordinary folk, but ignorance on the part of the medical profession about the microbes that caused all of those infections.

"Now Martha, I'm going to leave this bottle that I want you to use to keep little Billy's birth cord stump clean. Just apply some to a clean flannel cloth and dab it like this," he said, as he demonstrated.

As he continued his rounds he mentally thanked people like Joseph Lister, the Scottish professor of surgery who had introduced carbolic acid into medical and surgical practice, and Louis Pasteur and Robert Koch who had developed the Germ Theory and given doctors an understanding about the tiny organisms that caused all manner of infections.

George was glad that he lived in these exciting times with discoveries being made in laboratories around the world. He kept up to date with all the medical journals and tried to use each new advance in his Tombstone practice. And where he could, he tried his best to add to the advances of medicine and science in general.

Surgery was his main skill. He had been as successful in his surgical practice as anyone he had known and had contributed many papers to local, national and even international medical journals. Yet he found it amusing to think that so many of these discoveries had occurred in the short time since 1877 when silver prospector Ed Schieffelin had found silver where a friend had told him: "instead of a mine you'll find a tombstone."

That was how Tombstone had started, as a joke. Yet it was hardly a humorous place to life. It was a town that took itself deadly seriously on all levels. Fueled by silver mining, and the area was surrounded by mines, in the space of a mere decade it had grown to a population of more than 14,000. It had amenities aplenty as one would expect for such a fast-growing community. It had the Schieffelin Hall Opera House, four churches, a couple of banks, the growing newspaper empire of Stanley C. Bagg in the form of the *Tombstone Prospector* and the *Tombstone Epitaph*, the library, school and several clubs and societies for the gentler folk of the town. And for the less gentle, there were more than a hundred saloons, thirteen or fourteen gambling houses, a pool hall, a bowling alley, and the infamous

Bird Cage Theater, which was reported in the New York *Times* in 1881 to be the wildest and wickedest night spot between Basin Street and the Barbary Coast.

Apart from that there were many other places of entertainment of an even less salubrious nature, but which did a roaring trade and kept George and the other twelve doctors in Tombstone busy treating the diseases of Venus.

And it was certainly a serious place to live if you were intent on staying alive. The nature of mining towns was such that they attracted folks set upon enjoying the fruits of their toil. The town was like a magnet to scores of miners, cowboys and soldiers from nearby Fort Huachuca. Folks could get rowdy, drink themselves into ill tempers so that arguments or simple wanton behavior could be the result. Shootings were not uncommon, as was swift justice.

George knew this only too well and was reminded of it every time he passed a certain telegraph pole, which had been the scene of one particularly unpleasant act of rough justice in 1884, following what became known as the Bisbee Massacre. In December of 1883 five armed men attempted to rob the Goldwater & Castenada Store in nearby Bisbee, where four bystanders were killed. The authorities eventually tracked the gang of five down, together with John Heath, the man who masterminded it, but hadn't participated in the actual robbery, and put them in the Tombstone jail. At the trial the five men were sentenced to hang, but Heath was given a life sentence, a verdict that incensed the good folk of Tombstone and Bisbee. The result was that the jailor was overpowered by a mob and Heath was manhandled out of the jail and dragged to Toughnut Street where he was lynched on the telegraph pole and a placard was hung around his neck.

George had actually been a member of the posse that had gone in search of the gang when news of the massacre had reached Tombstone, so he was not entirely in sympathy with the victim of the necktie party. He was duly called as an expert medical witness at the subsequent inquest and opined that:

"He came to his death from emphysema of the lungs, a disease very common at high altitudes. In this case the disease was superinduced by strangulation, self-inflicted or otherwise."

As he walked up Second Street onto Allen Street he reflected on the other ghost-like memories of violent days in Tombstone. Many of them had occurred because the times were wild and the law was upheld in as forceful a manner as was deemed necessary. There was, of course, the Gunfight at the O.K. Corral back in 1881, the bloody debacle that everyone in town knew was bound to happen at some stage.

Virgil Earp was the Marshal of Tombstone at the time and he had deputized Morgan and Wyatt, his two brothers. Bad blood had developed between the Earps and two families, the Clantons and the McLaurys. The Earps believed the Clantons and McLaurys had rustled livestock out of Mexico. Not only that, but Wyatt was convinced that the Clantons had stolen a horse of his.

And of course, George remembered with a fond smile, there was Doc John Holliday, a good friend of Wyatt Earp, a dentist, gambler and consumptive rogue.

That fateful day in October had seen the deaths of Billy Clanton, Tom and Frank McLaury. Although his sympathies were with those of the Earps, George had attended once the shooting was over and tended the wounded of both factions. Young Billy Clanton, just 19 years old, had been shot in the wrist, chest and abdomen and was in mortal agony. George pulled the young cowboy's boots off because Billy had promised his mother that he would die with his boots off. It was about the only thing he could do for him.

Sheriff John Behan, who was no friend of the Earps, arrested them and Doc Holliday for murder, but after a trial that lasted thirty days, and included George's reports on the autopsies on Clanton and the two McLaury brothers, Judge

Wells Spicer, who happened to be kin to the Earps concluded that they had been justified in their actions and they were freed.

Then just after Christmas, Virgil had been gunned down on Fifth Street, between the Oriental Saloon and the Golden Eagle Brewery. Three men had blasted at him with shotguns from the cover of the adobe Huachuca Water Company building that was being erected. Virgil was badly wounded in the back and the upper left arm. It was a reprisal shooting for the O.K. Corral gunfight, that was clear.

George Parsons, George's best friend, had heard the shooting and gone to investigate, before dashing to the hospital to summon George to see him. Together they ran back to the Cosmopolitan Hotel where the wounded man had been taken, and where heavily armed Earp supporters were guarding his room. There they found Virgil covered in buckshot and with blood streaming from his arm wound and a lesser flesh wound on his left thigh. After examining him George had advised immediate amputation, but Virgil refused, saying he wanted to go to his grave with both arms.

With a wry smile George recalled Virgil stoically saying to his wife, who had been brought to him, that she must not worry, for he would still have one good arm to hug her with.

He was a stout fellow, Dr. Goodfellow thought,

recalling the operation the next day, when his fellow physician Doctor Henry Matthews had assisted him. He removed four inches of Virgil Earp's humerus to save the arm.

As he walked along the boardwalk in front of Campbell and Hatch's Saloon and Billiard Parlor, where he had earlier that morning operated on Red Douglas, the big Scottish immigrant miner, he reflected on how much drama that place had seen. And again, it was a place that had been heavily stained by the blood of one of the Earp family. In March 1882 he had been called urgently to minister to Morgan Earp who had been shot in the back through a back window of the parlor while he was playing pool with Bob Hatch himself.

George had felt bad that he couldn't do anything to help him, since Morgan was in a state of collapse from his wound by the time he saw him. His examination suggested that the bullet had entered his trunk to the left of the spinal cord, close to his kidney and exited from the front right side near his gall bladder. He died within three quarters of an hour.

Apart from the blood that was pumping out of the wounds he knew that death had been caused by the torrential hemorrhage inside Morgan's abdomen from the major vessels that had been damaged.

George had liked all of the Earp brothers,

especially Wyatt, although he sometimes had reservations about Wyatt's methods. Three days after Morgan's death the body of Frank Stillwell, who had been rumored to be seen running from the scene of the crime, was found near the railroad tracks.

He also recalled having to examine the body of Florentino Cruz, better known as Indian Charley, some months after Morgan's death, after he had been brought in by Wyatt and a posse after Wyatt had been appointed as a U.S. Deputy Marshal. He had four wounds on his body, one in the right temple, one in the right shoulder and two on the left. At least two of them were consistent with him having been shot when he was on his back. George suspected that Wyatt had taken no chance of him escaping justice.

George paid a visit to a guest at the Noble Hotel on Fremont Street. The man, a drummer of some sort, had been vomiting throughout the night causing Jackson Connors, the owner, some anxiety in case the man was going to complain that it was something to do with the dinner he had consumed in the restaurant the night before. George suspected that could well be the case, but so could an acute bout of drinking. There was an empty bottle of un-identifiable red eye whiskey on a table, which meant that he could have consumed any number of poisons in sufficient quantity to erode the lining of his stomach. He diagnosed acute gastritis and left a small bottle of bismuth to settle the man's stomach.

As he walked down Third Street he passed Camillus Fly's boarding house and picture studio. It was there that Doc John Holliday had stayed while he was living in Tombstone.

Holliday had been a real enigma, George mused. He was a cultured man yet when drunk he could be mean, spiteful and vicious. He was a dental surgeon by training, but a gambler by choice. And although slowly dying from tuberculosis he had come to the dry air of Tombstone to keep himself alive for as long as possible.

But now the Earps and Doc Holliday had all left Tombstone. Doc Holliday, like Morgan Earp, had shrugged off his mortal coil and had become merely another ghost memory. George had heard that he had died of his tuberculosis in Colorado in 1887 at the tender age of 36 years.

Holliday had actually consulted George about his tuberculosis months before the O.K. Corral gunfight. At the time George had believed as most of the medical profession had, that it was an inherited condition and that apart from living in a healthy climate and eating well, there wasn't a whole lot that could be done. Holliday had concurred with that view, since his own mother had suffered from the condition and died from it when he was just fifteen. George had realized that the cause was really very different when he read a paper written by Robert Koch in 1882, after Holliday had left for Colorado, in which the German doctor revealed that he had discovered the microbe that caused the condition.

Not that the knowledge would have done Holliday any good. There was knowing about something and there was being able to do something about it. George suspected that Holliday had been bent on living fast instead of dying slow.

George struck a light to his curly pipe and smoked it as he made his way to his last visit of the day at the Cochise County Hospital, where he had admitted Red Douglas the miner after his tracheotomy.

He had some knowledge of the big Scottish miner from past encounters with him in the Sonora minefields. George had interests in the Providencia Gold Mine, which he visited a couple of times a year. Red Douglas worked a claim in the vicinity and had a reputation as a fighter, having broken a fellow miner's jaw in an altercation fueled by poker and whiskey in one of the local cantinas.

George had been called upon to treat the man's jaw.

He intended to remind him about it if the big miner complained of his treatment when he saw him. He also intended to berate him for his foolish trick of putting a pool ball in his mouth.

"Doctor Goodfellow, I am afraid that you have had a wasted journey if you've come to see that big brute of a miner," said Sister Mary, who met him at the door. "He came around after a good two hours' deep sleep. He was like a bear with a sore head, which in a manner of speaking he was. He found the tracheotomy tube and ripped the stitches off and pulled the tube out." She held up a bowl containing the silver tube. "I've had it cleaned and soaked in carbolic acid, as you always insist."

"Damn it, he could have damaged the wound site!" George said. "Is he still in bed?"

"He's gone! He said he needed whiskey to kill the pain. Then he . . . he said he was going to find you and kill you!" She shuddered. "I was in two minds about sending for the marshal before you got here."

"Oh, he said that, did he?" George asked, two little patches of red showing on his cheeks. "Well, thank you, Sister," he said, as he opened his black bag and took out the wooden box that normally housed his tracheotomy tube. He replaced it and snapped the lid shut. "I'll go and see if I can find him. Did he say which saloon he was going to get whiskey from?"

"He did not," Sister Mary replied, looking quite concerned. "You are not seriously going to go and look for him, are you? He looks as if he could wrestle with a bear and come off best." She shook her head in exasperation. "Doctor Goodfellow, he said he was going to kill you!"

George Goodfellow's chin rose and his jaw set firmly. "He can try, Sister Mary. But not before I have given him my medical bill and made the ruffian pay it."

# Chapter 3
# SCIENCE IS THE KEY

Red Douglas was nowhere to be found. George started his search at Campbell and Hatch's Saloon and Billiard Parlor, where he asked the big miner's pool-playing friends who were still there where he was likely to be found. They listed half a dozen saloons, but no one had seen him since the drama of the morning.

George tried a few of the saloons before he gave up. Other than visiting the hundred or so others in Tombstone, he decided to just wait until Red Douglas showed up again. Apart from which, having had a whiskey in three of the saloons he had no wish to slow his reflexes any further.

He was actually very confident in his own ability to deal with most physical threats, having been the boxing champion at Annapolis, as well as having fought and won several fist fights in various mining camps earlier in his career. To win those unruly brawls simply meant being the last man standing.

Nevertheless, he was aware that the miner was a huge man with muscles hardened by a life of toil, so if needs be he would have no compunction about using the four-inch triple-edged Italian poniard that he habitually carried in a concealed sheath behind his back. He had used it a couple of years before and had been taken to court and fined $25 for stabbing Frank White after a fight occasioned by a heavy loss at cards the night before. George had consumed more whiskey than was good for him on that occasion, which was another reason for discontinuing his current search. He had enough insight to realize that whiskey had a tendency to bring out the worst in him and turn steadfastness into belligerence.

He reached under his coat and patted the poniard. Its presence reassured him as he walked home. Although he was calmness personified as he strutted along, swinging his bag in one hand and whistling a merry air, he was carefully watching every alleyway as he went, just in case Red Douglas should be lurking, waiting on his opportunity to make good his threat.

But there was no sudden attack. As would become apparent later, Red Douglas had left Tombstone to go off to let his wounded throat heal. His temper would be another matter.

It was mid-afternoon before he let himself into his house on First Street, which he had bought from Wyatt Earp when Wyatt left Tombstone for Albuquerque. It suited him well, since it was not far from his office and yet was far enough away from the rowdiness occasioned by the multiplicity of saloons. He especially liked it when Edith was staying with him, as she was at the moment.

Edith was twelve years old and the apple of George Goodfellow's eye. She had been badly upset by the death of her mother and so George had decided to keep her with him until the grieving was over. He was fortunate in having Stella Rimmington, Edith's old governess and now George's housekeeper and chief defender of his reputation. She had been widowed in her early twenties and had supported herself since then as a ladies' companion, children's governess and occasionally as a schoolteacher. She was now in her late forties and had worked and lived with the Goodfellows for twelve years, being employed by Katherine Goodfellow when she first became pregnant with Edith. Then as Katherine's health started to falter she became Edith's governess and when Edith went away to school she stayed on as George's housekeeper and cook.

Not a soul in Tombstone would have dared to cast any aspersions about the propriety of Dr. Goodfellow sharing a house with his housekeeper, for both of them were well known for their fire. George would counter any such slur with rhetoric or his fists if needs be, while Stella would not be averse to giving an offender a good tongue-lashing. It wasn't that Stella Rimmington wasn't an attractive woman, more that George

Goodfellow, who enjoyed female company well enough, made it a policy never to get involved with either patients or employees.

"Daddy, come quick," Edith called from the back of the house as George let himself in, stowed his medical bag on the hall stand and hung his hat up. "Lucrezia looks poorly."

Stella Rimmington appeared from the kitchen door. "She's been worrying all morning, Doctor Goodfellow, sir," she stated formally, the way she always addressed him, since that was her way of maintaining strict boundaries between them. "Although how she can tell one of those ugly creatures from the other, is beyond me."

"They all have their own distinct features and their own personalities, Stella. I have told you before."

Stella stood wiping her hands on her apron. "I am not convinced about that, Doctor, just as I am not convinced that it is safe to have a dozen of these Gila Monsters living with people."

"Daddy, can you come and look at her . . . please?"

"Coming, Edith, my dear," he replied.

Then to Stella: "They are not exactly living with us, Stella. They are all of them housed in their own enclosures. Which again is how Edith can tell them apart."

"But they are poisonous, Doctor! Everyone knows that. Your friend Doctor Handy from

Tucson told me that when he was last here."

"I am not sure that he exactly meant that, Stella. I think he may have meant that bites from them can go septic. The same applies to any kind of bite."

"I am sure that he said they were poisonous, Doctor. Anyway, surely it is not a good idea to let a young girl like Edith get too close to them? They are not proper pets for a young girl. They ... they are bound to bring bad luck."

George gave a harrumph of irritation. If there was one thing that annoyed him about Stella it was her tendency to be superstitious. "They are not her pets, Stella. They are all my specimens in a study I am making of them. It is called science. It's the key to learning."

Edith popped her head around the back door. "Daddy, I am really worried."

George lost his irritation immediately when he saw his daughter. She had her mother's sparkling eyes and a pretty, smiling mouth that never failed to melt his heart.

He laughed and crossed to the door to give her an affectionate tousle of the hair. "Lead the way, Edith, my dear."

She responded by giving him a hug before immediately turning on her heel and dashing out. George followed her outside to the back yard, in an area of which George had employed Zach Donoghue, a carpenter and housepainter, to section off into a dozen four-by-four foot enclosures, each with a five feet high wall, containing its own pile of stones arranged inside like a mini cave and with sufficient room for the Gila Monsters to dig burrows or to bask in the sun if they had a mind to. Zach had built them well so that they were escape proof, yet with holes high up on the fences for Edith to view them through.

George had always encouraged Edith to be enquiring and to develop a scientific mind, like his own. And in this he had been successful, for her greatest joy was in reading and doing experiments. Her favorite book was a leather-bound volume of *The Magic of Science: A Manual of Easy and Instructive Scientific Experiments*, by James Wylde. It was an old book published in 1861, that George had been given when he was a ten-year-old youngster by his father, Milton Goodfellow. Milton Goodfellow had been a Forty-Niner and professional mining engineer who had been educated at Allegheny College in Pennsylvania, where he had taken classes in medicine and dentistry along with his mining studies. With his love of science and learning and a smattering of medicine, the senior Goodfellow was also always referred to as Dr. Goodfellow.

The love of science and experimentation had filtered through the three generations.

Ever since Dr. John Handy had described the

case of his Gila-bitten patient a few months before when he had visited George from Tucson to discuss a number of shared medical interests, and expounded on his view that they were poisonous, George had passionately thrown himself into studying Gila Monsters. He doubted that they were poisonous to humans and thought that they merited further study.

As he always did when he decided to do something, he did it without sparing a thought of expense. He offered locals five dollars a specimen, the result being his significant collection of Gilas, ranging from nine to a couple of dozen inches in length. He found the orange, yellow and black beaded–scale reptiles quite fascinating.

And Edith had named each and every one of them. Despite the fact that George tried to persuade her to name them simply, she had chosen names that were in keeping with the Gila Monsters' supposedly toxic nature. He supposed that Stella had assisted her in either giving them the names of various poisoners from history, or the names of their victims. Hence her two favorites were Lucrezia, a large, coral pink, plump bodied specimen two feet long named after Lucrezia Borgia, and Socrates, a smaller yellow and black fellow of a mere twelve inches, named after the ancient Greek philosopher who had drunk a cup of hemlock.

Edith hopped onto a wooden box that she used to reach the viewing peephole in Lucrezia's enclosure fence. "See Daddy, she's just lying there half in and half out of her cave. I think she looks sick and she's barely moving."

George looked over the fence and laughed. "I think she's fine, Edith. She's just sleeping it off."

"Sleeping what off, Daddy?"

"Her meal. I put two mice in there this morning. She's just digesting. That's enough food for her for a week or so. Look!" And he clapped his hands, the result being that Lucrezia disdainfully got up and shuffled around into her cave of stones. "She was just lying in the sun."

George chuckled and went around the other enclosures and checked a couple of the other inmates of his Gila zoo, who happened also to be basking rather than resting inside their burrows as Gila Monsters were wont to do in the heat of the day.

"And in fact, I think that's quite what I'd like to do before we sample the delicious cake that Stella seems to be baking for us."

"You want to lie out in the sun?" Edith asked with a puzzled expression that made her nose wrinkle most attractively. It was another feature that she had inherited from her mother.

"No, not out in the sun, but I'd quite like to lie down and take a nap before we have coffee and cake."

Edith jumped on the box to look at Lucrezia again. She heaved a sigh of relief. "I'm glad she'll be all right. I still can't believe that they don't need to drink the way that all other creatures do."

"I told you, Edith, that's because they are adapted to survive. They get the water they need from their prey and they store up fat in their tails."

Edith jumped down and took his hand. "Can we go to the Snake Ranch soon? I'd like to see what my brands look like on my cattle."

George laughed and squeezed her little hand. "Maybe soon, when my practice gets a little less busy."

A few months ago, when his wife Katherine's health was taking a turn for the worse over in Oakland where his mother lived, he had registered a brand in Edith's name, for his cattle on the Snake Ranch that he co-owned over Sonora way. Every few months he tried to go over and inspect things, combining it with a trip to oversee his share of the nearby Providencia Gold Mine.

He was just leading the way inside, playfully swinging Edith's arm back and forth when he heard Stella talking to someone at the front door. His heart sank slightly, for he knew that it was likely to be a request to see a patient. And that would mean no nap, and possibly no cake.

George recognized the voice of Carlton Levine, the head schoolteacher of the Tombstone School.

"Carlton, can I help you?" he asked.

"Mister Levine was just telling me that his wife is ill," Stella said. "He was wondering if you could call on her. I told him that we would be having coffee and cake soon."

George clicked his tongue. "It's been a busy day, Carlton, but I'm here and listening. Come into the parlor and tell me what's wrong. Maybe Stella will serve us all some cake."

Carlton Levine was as tall as George and just a couple of years younger. He had a kindly face crowned by a mop of curly black hair. He was well-liked by the pupils of the school and by their parents who all felt that he was giving them as good an education as they could possibly expect without sending their youngsters off to an expensive fee-paying school back East. That was in fact precisely what the Goodfellows had done with Edith, yet it had never affected George's relationship with Carlton Levine, for he was aware that the Goodfellows had been cautious about Edith's health ever since their son, little George junior had died in infancy back in 1882. George had told him about it.

"To be honest, George, if you don't mind, I'd just as soon not come in. If there is any chance of you coming to see her straight away, I would appreciate it."

George nodded and reached for his medical bag and his hat. "Lead on, Carlton."

As they walked up First Street and along Safford Street towards the Levines' two story house on the other side of the road from St Paul's Episcopal Church, George quizzed the schoolteacher.

"So what's been the trouble?"

"Esme's in agony, George. I've never seen her like this. She had been feeling a bit queasy at breakfast and felt a bit worse at lunchtime. I didn't think too much about it then, but when I got home after school she was vomiting and she's been doubled up with stomach pains."

"How have you felt yourself?"

"Fine. We've eaten the same meals, so I don't think it can be anything she ate."

A few minutes later George was sitting at Esme Levine's bedside, taking a medical history while her husband stood anxiously at the threshold.

"So it's pain that comes in spasms and you've been sick four or five times?" he recapped.

Esme Levine was a pretty blonde-haired woman of thirty-one years who had come to Tombstone with her husband in 1887 when he had been appointed head schoolteacher at the age of twenty-nine. She had also been a teacher, but when they came to Tombstone they had decided that she would not work, but would give private lessons in art and be at home to support Carlton.

The walls of the bedroom were covered with impressive samples of her artwork.

George had seen her professionally on a couple of occasions and knew that her health was fragile, rather as his own wife Katherine's had been. He also suspected that she may have been trying to conceive a child and had been finding it hard to do.

"That's right, Doctor Goodfellow. I . . . I feel so thirsty as well." She looked up at her husband. "Carlton, could you get me a glass of water, please?"

While Carlton was out of the room George examined her. She watched his face as he palpated her abdomen.

"What is it?" she asked anxiously as she saw his eyebrows rise momentarily.

"When was your last monthly show, Esme?"

She took a sharp intake of breath and shook her head. "No! No! That's not right. It . . . it's impossible."

Carlton came back in the room with the glass of water. "What's impossible, Esme?"

George saw the look of panic in her eyes. He assumed it was not the right moment for a discussion. He needed time to talk with his patient and the best way was to do it alone.

"I haven't finished my examination yet, Carlton. I need to perform a more intimate examination, so maybe you could give us ten minutes?"

Carlton glanced at his wife. She sipped water then nodded.

"Please Carlton, let Doctor Goodfellow do what he needs to do."

"Well, as it happens, I need to collect some things from school for The Microscopical Society meeting tonight. You're coming, aren't you, George?"

George had been the secretary of the local science and philosophical club since the early '80s and had given several lectures on a variety of his medical, scientific and geological studies. "God willing, I'll be there. You're talking tonight about chess, aren't you."

"That's right, about Checkers, Chess and Chase Board games, actually. I need to pick up some of the games I had been using to teach the children about tactics. Games are a good way of keeping hold of the children's interest." He smiled. "It'll take me about ten minutes." He bent down and gave his wife a chaste kiss on the cheek. "I'll be back then, my dear."

Esme Levine patted the back of his hand and gave him a winsome smile. "I'll be fine, Carlton," she said. "I'm sure I'll be fine."

After performing an internal examination and then going to wash his hands, George returned to the bedroom and sat down beside the bed.

"I thought you might be pregnant."

"I sort of realized that. That's why I said it was impossible."

"Why were you so sure?"

"Because we haven't . . . we haven't lain together like a husband and wife in over a year."

"Your abdomen feels like it has a sixteen week pregnancy, but after doing the internal examination I know that you are not pregnant."

Her eyes grew wide with alarm.

"Esme, you have a tumor in your abdomen. It may be what we call a fibroid, or it could be . . ."

"What? It could be what?" she asked urgently.

George wished that her husband would return. He felt that he should know about this.

"Please tell me before Carlton comes back."

"It may be quite benign. It could be a growth on the womb called a fibroid, or a cyst coming from an ovary. But it is also possible that it could be a malignant tumor."

Esme Levine gasped and slumped backwards against the bank of pillows. "What can be done, Doctor?"

"Esme, I might be able to do an operation called a hysterectomy, that involves opening your abdomen and removing the tumor and probably most of your womb as well. It would be a difficult and dangerous operation and I would need at least another doctor to help me."

Tears were rolling down her cheeks. "I had

always hoped to have children. That is, until . . . until . . ."

"What has happened, Esme? I and others had always assumed that you and Carlton were just having trouble starting a family."

"We've been having troubles, since he started . . ." She had been looking down at her hands, but now she looked at him and wiped her eyes. "I don't want to talk about it. It would be . . . it would be disloyal."

Suddenly, she grabbed her abdomen and her face creased in pain. "Is . . . is this causing the pain."

"I think so. I think it is twisting on itself. When that happens it cuts off its own blood supply and causes spasms."

He could see that she was going to vomit and managed to get a bowl for her just in time.

"If we are going to do this operation, it will have to be soon, Esme. We can't delay, in case it is malignant."

She accepted the towel that he offered her to dab her mouth. "I need to think about it, Doctor Goodfellow. It's not an easy thing to understand. I don't want you to say anything to Carlton. Can you just give me something to stop being sick and help the pain?"

"He should know, Esme."

Her eyes were dry now and in her steely look he recognized a firm resolve.

"It is my body, Doctor, and that is my decision."

George stood up. "Well, I wish I understood, but my Hippocratic Oath doesn't allow me to go against your wishes."

The outside door opened and closed and moments later Carlton Levine came in. His face looked hopeful.

"Well, George, will she be all right?"

Esme interrupted. "Everything will be just fine, Carlton. It will just take a few days and Doctor Goodfellow is going to give me some medicine to ease this pain." She forced a smile. "That's right, isn't it, Doctor."

George was reluctant to tell a lie, but neither was he prepared to break his Hippocratic Oath and divulge anything against her wishes. "Yes, I'm going to my office to make up some medicine right away. And I'll keep an eye on Esme over the next few days."

At least I'm not telling a lie there, he thought to himself.

Carlton looked relieved. "Excellent. Then I'll come back with you and wait while you make the medicine up. I have to get my lovely wife on her feet again."

George nodded as he packed his medical bag. He needed to know what Esme Levine was keeping from him. Then maybe he could get her to see reason about having surgery.

Back in the dispensing room at George's

office, Carlton watched the doctor as he expertly prepared two bottles of medicine. One he labeled *Bismuthi Subcarbonas* and the other *Laudanum et Asafoetidae.*

"I want you to give her the Bismuthi Subcarbonas in a little milk every two hours. The doses are on the label, and then give the Laudanum et Asafoetidaeone teaspoonful every four hours. The first will ease the nausea and the second will kill the pain. Don't give too much of the Laudanum mixture or else the Asafetida in it will make the nausea worse."

"Medicine is a fine balancing art, isn't it, George," Carlton said admiringly. "It amazes me the way you can keep all of those medicine formulae in your head. And this place is as good a laboratory as they have at the assayer's office."

George slapped his friend on the back. "Well, let's hope it does its job. You start giving that to Esme and I'll drop by and see her tomorrow."

It was only when the schoolteacher had gone that George realized how hungry he felt.

Stella had laid out a light snack of sandwiches and cake for him and Edith was already sitting at the table when he came in.

"Thank goodness you're back," Stella said. "There's bad news. A telegram just arrived from Tucson for you and I opened it. You're going to have to eat your supper quick."

George picked up the small yellow envelope where she had placed it by his place setting. He opened it and read:

> Come at once. Hurry. Doctor Handy shot by Frank Heney in Tucson. The rail yard is sending an extra to Benson for you. Get there quickly.
> Dr. Michael Spencer

"Damn!" he cursed as he folded it and put it in a pocket.

"What's wrong, Daddy?" Edith asked, looking up at him in amazement, for he never swore in front of her.

"My friend Doctor Handy has been shot. I'll have to go to Tucson and see him."

"Can I come, too, Daddy? I like Doctor Handy."

George shook his head. "No, Edith, my dear. I'm going to have to get to Benson as fast as I can. I'll have to go on El Rosillo."

Stella was standing, shaking her head. "And we were just talking about Doctor Handy and those poisonous creatures today. I said it was an omen. A bad omen."

# Chapter 4
## HASTE

El Rosillo was a fine horse and George Goodfellow was used to riding long distances to see patients. Ordinarily he would go by horse and buggy, using Lucy-May, his other horse, but when he needed to travel fast he opted for the horse that had been given to him by the Mexican president Porfirio Diaz. He loaded up his specially designed G. W. Elliott saddlebags, which had compartments for his portable carbolic spray, his surgical instruments, chloroform, suture materials, diagnostic equipment and medicines, as well as room for shaving tackle and a change of clothes, and as usual when he was travelling alone, he carried a Navy Colt revolver and a Winchester in the scabbard.

El Rosillo covered the ground from Tombstone to Benson as quickly as George considered it safe to do so. He had no wish to exhaust the animal, nor to strand himself on the open trail miles from anywhere.

At the depot he found that a Southern Pacific engine was steamed up and ready for him. It consisted only of the engine, coal bin and a caboose.

A group of men were huddled around the platform waiting for him.

A thin man dressed in a conductor's uniform detached himself from the group.

"Doctor Goodfellow, I'm Joe Scott and I'd like to welcome you aboard this extra. The Company has impressed on us that we are to get you to Tucson in all haste. Will you join me in the caboose? I can make you as comfortable as possible."

"I thank you, Joe, but I've been sitting in a saddle for too long and I need to stretch my legs."

He dismounted and pulled off his saddlebags.

"We'll see to your horse, Doctor," a man wearing an eyeshade and gartered sleeves said. "Meanwhile, here's a telegram for you."

George read it. It was another from Dr Michael Spencer.

> Dr. Handy slipping away. Shot in the abdomen at 3 o'clock. Any instructions?

"Damn!" he cursed as he folded it and stuffed it in a pocket with the other telegram.

"Any message, Doctor?" the telegrapher asked.

"Yes. Say: Give no water and start praying. If he's failing, then operate!"

As the telegrapher headed off to send the message George handed his saddlebag to the brakeman, who had introduced himself as Sandy Reynolds. "Don't jostle that any," he instructed. "There are precious bottles in there."

The conductor held his hand out in the direction of the caboose. "There's plenty room to stretch your legs in the caboose, Doctor Goodfellow."

"No, I'll ride up in the cab," George said. "I need to get to Tucson as quick as we can and I'd like to see how we're going. Speed is of the essence and a man's life is hanging in the balance here."

Two grinning faces looked down at him as he climbed the step up to the cab.

"I'm Grover Brown, the engineer, and this is Jim Moody the fireman. We'll do our best to get you to Tucson as fast as possible, Doctor Goodfellow. We both know Doctor Handy."

The shorter of the two men nodded effusively. "And we've both heard of you, Doc. If anyone can help him it's you."

"Well, let's get going boys. Literally every minute counts."

As the extra hurtled along, George smoked his pipe and quizzed Grover Brown about the operation of the engine. Every now and then he pulled out his hunter watch and stared at it as if wishing to speed up the process. His conversation grew increasingly terse.

"I need you to get this engine going much faster, boys," he said as they approached Mescal.

"I'm going as fast as I can coax her, Doctor," replied Grover Brown.

"The hell you are," George said. "Now step back and let me in there." He pulled the startled engineer back and took his place. "This throttle can open up a whole lot more," he said as he opened it up to its limit.

The engine responded and soon they were accelerating on the downward tracks towards Tucson.

"Just keep stoking and we'll get there fine and dandy," cried the doctor, his eyes seeming to blaze.

The next twenty miles were covered in as many minutes, causing Joe Scott the conductor and Sandy Reynolds the brakeman in the caboose much anxiety.

"You're going to need to put on the brakes a mite, Sandy," Joe said. "This patch is getting too dangerous at this speed. What in thunder is Grover playing at?"

"It isn't him at the throttle," said Sandy. "It's Doc Goodfellow."

"That's even worse. He's no engineer. I'm putting on the handbrake now."

But when he pulled the handbrake all that happened was that the wheels let out an enormous squeal, like a dozen animals in pain.

"Darn it, Joe. You're the conductor and I'm the brakeman. You can't do that. You don't know about braking, just like the doc don't know about driving."

"I've got to. At this speed we're all going to get to the next life ten years early instead of making Tucson ten minutes faster."

"Let it go, Joe. The wheels will just lock and at this speed there'll be nothing holding us on the track. That's the surest way to get this train to crash."

In the cab Dr. Goodfellow had demanded Grover and Jim explain what the squealing noise was.

"That'll be Joe and Sandy applying the handbrake. They think we're going too fast, too."

Goodfellow's jaw lifted belligerently and the engineer expected to hear a stream of invective. But the squealing stopped and the engine carried on unimpeded, picking up speed again.

When they finally arrived at Tucson at 8:15 pm everyone was amazed to discover that they had covered the 46 mile journey in record time.

"Thank you, gentlemen, I appreciate the effort you took to get me here as quickly as possible."

George took his G. W. Elliott saddlebags and went straight for the buggy that was ready and waiting to take him to Dr. Handy's house. He was quite happy for Grover Brown to bask in the glory and claim the record time.

It was exactly 8:30 pm by the time George arrived at Dr. John C. Handy's house. He had been there many times, for he and Dr. Handy had much in common. Dr. Handy was nine years older than George and in a way had been something of a mentor to him when he first came to Arizona. The two men were both considered to have bullish natures and yet both had been more than moderately successful.

Both of them had been contract surgeons in their early careers and both had fiery tempers that had caused them trouble at times in their lives. In Handy's case, however, that anger had been either directed at or caused by the women that he had gotten close to.

George had heard about Handy's early life from colleagues. He had been the contract surgeon at US Army Camp Thomas, where he married a young Apache woman. He had been besotted by her, but when the post trader started paying her undue attentions, they had a disagreement and Handy killed him. He was arrested, of course, but acquitted of all charges. Unfortunately, it soured his relationship with his wife and they were summarily divorced.

But then when he moved to Tucson in 1871 and set up his shingle, he remarried a young woman called Mary Page. His treatment of her, by all accounts, was brutal and included chaining her to her bed for days at a time and feeding her morphine until she became dependent upon both the drug and him as a supplier of it!

George knew that Handy had a roving eye despite his marriage. And yet he was professionally well respected as the attending physician at St. Mary's Hospital as well as having the busiest private practice in Tucson. Not only that, but in 1886 he was appointed as the first Chancellor of the University of Arizona. Yet there again his temper betrayed him and after arguments with the university board he was removed from office after a mere six months.

As he knocked on the door, George wondered whether that temper of Handy's had something to do with the shooting.

The door was opened and a man of similar age to George, with a handlebar mustache and receding hair admitted him.

"Ah, George, thank heavens you have arrived," said Dr. Hiram Fenner. "Michael Spencer and John Green are in the parlor. We've been taking it in turns to keep an eye on the patient."

The two doctors shook hands. George knew and liked Hiram Fenner, albeit he considered him an eccentric. He specialized in tubercular patients and was making a name for himself by treating them with juices of various vegetables. He was also famous in the region as the owner of the first steam-car, which he called his Locomobile, and which he had crashed into a giant saguaro on its maiden outing.

George followed him through to the parlor

where two men were sitting smoking cigars. Neither seemed to be enjoying them.

"Ah, Goodfellow," said a short man with a spade-like beard. "We've been waiting for you."

Goodfellow shook Dr. John Trail Green's hand and nodded as the third man stood up and offered his hand. He was a tall, clean-shaven man with wire-framed spectacles perched on a thin nose.

"We did as much as we dared," said Dr. Michael Spencer, "but we fear it's not enough."

"Sit down, George," said Dr. Hiram Fenner. "A few more minutes won't hurt and it's as well if we filled you in on the background to this affair."

George slumped into a chair and pulled out his pipe and started filling it from a battered leather pouch. "Some coffee and a bite to eat wouldn't go amiss either, if that is possible, gentlemen. I've had a long horse ride and a longer, if exhilarating train journey."

"I'll get some bread and cheese," said Dr. Green. "Handy's wife isn't here, which is half the problem as you'll hear."

"I heard that he'd filed for divorce," George said, striking a light to his pipe and puffing blue smoke ceilingwards.

"As a matter of fact, it was his wife Mary who first of all filed for divorce," said Hiram. "But she retracted it when John Handy put pressure on her. To tell you the truth, he also threatened to kill Judge Sloan and any lawyers who took on her case. Then he sent his children off to stay with his mother and his sister. You know what a temper he has."

"Never been on the end of it myself," George commented, "but I've heard."

Hiram went on: "Well, then a couple of years ago he filed for divorce. The talk around town is that he wanted to be free to go off with a young woman called Pansy Smith. He got the court's permission to take his young son into hospital care."

Michael Spencer leaned forward and rested his hands on his knees. "I'm afraid that Mary Handy had trouble getting a lawyer to represent her, because John Handy successfully intimidated the legal profession in Tucson. Eventually she got Frank Heney to take her case on, but Handy threatened to kill him. He made it known to everyone that she was an opium fiend and an unfit mother and he laid it on thick that he was the long-suffering poor husband. But when Heney didn't back down and then didn't rise to Handy's threats and attempts to goad him into a fight, he started to get really vindictive. Believe it or not but he actually tried to ride him down in his buggy. Anyway they went to trial and it dragged on and on for months, until he got custody of all of the children. Then he tried to have her thrown out of her house, saying that she had made it over to him. Again, Frank Heney acted for her. And again, Handy threatened to kill him. That was when Frank Heney started to carry a gun with him."

Dr. Green returned with a tray with a plate of bread and cheese and a pot of coffee.

"Ah, food!" George exclaimed, leaning forward to help himself. "It sounds like something bad was bound to happen."

"And it did," said Hiram. "At noon today Handy waylaid Heney in the street, pushed him against a wall and struck him in the face. Heney pulled his gun and tried to back away, but Handy tried to take the gun off him. They grappled and by all accounts the gun just went off. Deputy Sheriff John Wiegle and a bunch of others managed to get the gun away. Somehow Handy managed to make his way to his office and Michael and I were called in."

"Heney was arrested," Dr. Green volunteered, "but it is likely he will get bail."

Dr. Fenner went on:

"Michael and I examined John. The bullet had gone almost straight through his abdomen. He was in agony, of course. It was lodged close to his spine and we could see it bulging through the skin. So we managed to make an incision and remove it in his office. And then we brought him home, thinking he'd be more comfortable here."

"Then we all examined him again and agreed

with him that we should send for you," added Michael Spencer. "He's in a bad way, George."

"Does he know that?" George asked.

"He does. He had his lawyer with him this afternoon and he's remade his will. But he's hopeful that you'll be able to save him."

George took out his watch and glanced at it. "So it's been almost nine hours since he was shot." He sucked air between his teeth and then took a final gulp of coffee. "Gentlemen, I think it's time I saw the patient."

Dr. John Handy was lying back against a bank of pillows looking exhausted and in considerable pain. He had a full head of black hair and a full beard. His face was bathed in perspiration and his eyes seemed sunken into their sockets.

"George . . . thank the Lord . . . that you've come."

"I came as soon as I could, John. I was shocked to hear that you had been shot."

"That cur of a lawyer Frank Heney killed me, George." He pointed weakly at the three other doctors who had come in after George and stationed themselves at the end of the bed. "That's what I and our friends here think."

"You're not dead yet, old friend. That's why I'm here. We've got to get you back on your feet so you can get on with healing the sick."

George saw the glimmer of hope flash across his colleague's face. He tried to be as positive as he could, despite the fact that he was concerned about the time that had elapsed since the shooting.

"If you get me back on my feet, George Goodfellow, I'll buy you a crate of the best whiskey in the world. To tell you the truth . . . it's . . . it's my youngsters that I'm more concerned about than my patients. They . . . need me."

George turned to Hiram. "So you and Michael removed the bullet. What caliber was it?"

"It was a .32," Hiram Fenner replied.

"That is the first piece of good news," George said with a nod. "As I'm sure you will all know, if you read my paper on the management of gunshot wounds in the *Southern California Practitioner*, a couple of years back, the caliber of the weapon is crucial in abdominal wounds."

"I read it, George," Dr. Handy said, weakly. "But the bloody fool shot me as I was trying to take the gun from him. It . . . it was pressed up close to me when it went off."

George sat down and gently pulled back the bed covers and removed the thick dressings. He maintained a professionally calm countenance even though he was aware Handy understood that a close-up wound would bring additional problems.

And as he inspected the wound his suspicions were confirmed. There were significant burns around the entry wound in the lower abdomen. The wound was already tumescent, red and swollen.

"There is a second good bit of news, John," he said reassuringly to Dr. Handy. "It's a lower abdominal wound. That makes it less likely to have damaged the liver or the kidneys."

"Or the spleen," offered Dr. John Green.

"If the spleen had been hit then death would have been damned near instant," George replied without looking around. "The spleen hemorrhages catastrophically."

He laid a hand on Handy's abdomen and gently palpated, all the time watching the pain that it elicited on the patient's face. Then he placed his left hand flat on the abdomen and percussed the back of the middle finger with the tip of his right middle finger. He nodded as he listened to the sound that it produced.

"Let's see what I can hear now," he said, pulling out his stethoscope and uncoiling the rubber tubing. He placed the earpieces in his ears and listened at several points on the abdomen as he moved the funnel around.

"There are not a lot of borborygmi there. That might mean that the intestine that isn't damaged is already paralyzed. And on percussion it is clear that there is a lot of blood in the abdomen. We're going to have to operate on you, John. And as soon as we can."

"Good . . . but I can't say that I . . . re . . . relish being put to sleep with chloroform."

"I'll happily see to the anesthetic, Doctor Handy," John Green volunteered. "I've used it a lot and I have a Chisolm chloroform inhaler, which means I can reduce the dose that you need to a single drachm. That will be an eighth of the dose that you need by the traditional method. The benefit is that you won't get any of the suffocative side effects that you get with the old way of dripping onto a face mask."

Handy gave a nod of relief. "I thank you, John. The Chisolm inhaler is the finest medical invention to come from the days of the Confederacy."

"Right then, gentlemen," George said, as he stood up. "The anesthetic is settled. Dr Green will do it. Are you happy for me to operate?"

"We are," replied Hiram Fenner. "And we are both happy to assist you at the operation."

"Well, in fact I'd like just one of you to assist and one to operate my carbolic spray. We need a fine spray onto the operation site throughout the procedure. I have a small portable machine that I had built according to Professor Lister's design."

"Hiram is your assistant then, George," Dr. Spencer said. "I'll do the spraying."

"And we have the kitchen table already scrubbed and ready," Dr. Green announced.

It was ten past ten that night before the four doctors had the kitchen transformed into an operating theater.

Dr. Handy shook hands with each of them and said a prayer before Dr. Green administered the chloroform via the Chisolm inhaler that consisted of a small brass box with two tubes, one of which was inserted up each nostril.

"Just breathe in and out through your nose, John," he urged the patient. "If you get a tightening feeling in the back of the throat, just open your mouth and breathe in and out. That'll take away any unpleasant sensations."

And within a few moments Dr. John Handy was asleep.

George instructed Michael Spencer on the operation of the carbolic spray, which consisted of a metal cylinder containing a water bath above a spirit lamp, with tubes leading to and from a bottle containing carbolic acid. The water was boiled to produce steam, which was then pumped by hand into the carbolic acid, which was taken up by the steam and emitted into the air as a spray.

"Keep it topped up and just keep that spray above the operation."

Then George and Spencer washed their hands

in carbolic and soaked all of the instruments.

"Now gentlemen," George said, as he pointed his chin at the clock. "It is precisely 10:20 pm. Let us proceed with as much haste as we dare."

Before he operated on a gunshot wound George always made it a point to try to work out the track of the bullet, thereby having a good idea of what anatomical structures could be damaged.

In John Handy's case the wound had entered one inch below and to the left of the umbilicus. The wound on his back, from whence Drs. Fenner and Spencer had extracted the bullet, was almost directly opposite it. This, George deduced, meant that the gun had been pointing directly at his abdomen, which was better than had it been pointing upwards, for that would surely have hit major organs and probably been fatal already.

He made an extended incision parallel with the linea alba and just an inch lateral to the swollen and inflamed wound.

Immediately, blood started to spurt from the abdomen and together, George and Hiram Fenner started to soak it up and remove blood clots and intestinal contents from the cavity.

"Keep that spray going, Michael," George urged. "With this much intestinal ooze we're going to have to make sure that we get his peritoneum as clean as possible."

Then slowly and methodically George started

to examine the small intestine. He found eighteen separate perforations.

The three Tucson doctors watched with admiration as he skillfully worked on the damaged intestines.

"I always use the glover's stitch on intestinal wounds," he explained as he executed a continuous lock-stitch suture by each time passing the needle through the loop of the preceding stitch.

"Whereas interrupted stitches are fine for other tissues, because the intestine is so vascular, you have to make sure that you have as hemostatic a closure as possible. That way you are also less likely to get further ooze of intestinal fluid into the abdominal cavity."

None of the three doctors raised an objection to George's lecturing manner, for they were all too well aware that he was the expert in gunshot surgery and was pushing back the frontiers of surgical practice all the time. Even some of the forceps that he was using to control bleeding were instruments of his own design, made for him by Tiemann & Co of New York.

They had been operating for almost three hours and all had seemed to be going well. George was enjoying the surgical challenge and was starting to feel a glow of satisfaction as he approached the end of the operation.

He had just closed the very last perforation

when Dr. Green cursed and held his small mirror close to the patient's mouth. There was no misting of its surface. Then he felt for a pulse.

"I am sorry, Doctors," he said, shaking his head. "Our patient has just died."

It was quarter past one in the morning.

# Chapter 5
# FRUSTRATION

George barely slept that night. Like the other three doctors he was frustrated and felt that he had failed his colleague.

They had tended to Dr. Handy's body then arranged for one of the attendants who had been waiting to sit with the patient after the operation to go and fetch the undertaker.

Then they had returned to Dr. Fenner's house where they drank a toast to their dead colleague.

"We were too late!" George said as they sat around Dr. Fenner's dining room table, with a decanter of whiskey in the middle. "It was just as I said in my paper, any abdominal wound with a caliber of .32 or more should be operated on within an hour."

"That wasn't possible, George," said Hiram. "We got you here as soon as humanly possible. None of us had the expertise to perform an operation like that."

George grunted and struck a light to his pipe. "Do any of you gentlemen enjoy poetry?"

"I do," replied Michael Spencer. "Have you a poem in mind to help think about John Handy?"

George blew out a thin stream of smoke. "No,

I was thinking more about how I feel about not saving him. There is a line from *Endymion*, by the English poet John Keats. It goes: 'There is not a fiercer hell than the failure in a great object.' That is how it feels to me, gentlemen. This feels like hell. We tried and we failed to keep one of our own profession alive."

Hiram Fenner sighed and looked at the crestfallen faces around the table. He reached for the decanter. "I think we could all do with another drink, gentlemen."

He poured each a generous measure then raised his glass.

"I propose another toast—to John Handy, who knew that we were all trying to do our best for him."

George had always been able to hold his liquor and still work the next day. Drs. Green and Spencer were not so sure that they had a similar capacity. Nor did they have much inclination to drown their sorrows at having lost a colleague.

Hiram Fenner had one final drink with George before retiring to join his wife in their marital bed. Before he did, he showed George the guest room where it had been arranged for him to stay.

"My house is your house, George. Help yourself to anything you want to eat or drink. I'm hoping that we'll all feel a mite better in the morning."

"We are professionals, Hiram. That is the nature of our profession, you win some and you lose some."

George sat in the parlor smoking his pipe while he drank the rest of the decanter. Then feeling only partially satiated he found a bottle of brandy in a cabinet and a box of cigars.

It was four o'clock by the time he finally went to bed having consumed half the bottle and smoked four of Hiram's cigars. Unfortunately, neither the spirits nor the tobacco had made him feel a bit better.

Inevitably, he barely slept at all, for his mind kept berating him for failing to keep John Handy alive.

"You are a damned useless fool, George Goodfellow," he mumbled to himself as he lay alone in the darkness. "Tucson has lost one hell of a good doctor, thanks to you! Why the hell didn't you ride faster or get that darned train to really travel? And then you sat down and filled your stomach with bread and cheese instead of seeing the patient and operating straight away."

And then he fell into a doze, a fitful slumber wherein his mind kept replaying the journey on El Rosillo, then the hell-for-leather train journey from Benson to Tucson.

"Too slow," he mumbled in his sleep. "Too darned slow."

With which he woke himself and punched the

pillow in frustration. "Tarnation! John Handy had no chance of surviving because of those ten hours between the shooting and the moment I made the incision at the start of the operation."

The one question that never occurred to him was whether any of the Tucson doctors should have operated on their colleague. He was too well aware that none of them had the surgical skill to perform such a procedure.

"Damn it! I was so close. So close!"

El Rosillo had been happy to see him when he arrived back at Benson. He nuzzled George's shoulders when he turned to lift his saddlebags up. Then he nickered.

"And I am sure pleased to see you, too. It's been a tough and sad time and I am pleased to see a familiar, happy face."

Although he was conscious that there was a lot of work waiting for him when he got back to Tombstone, he was feeling less than enthusiastic. The slight muzzy hangover from his drinking the night before was no problem, for it was something that he often had when he over imbibed at the Crystal Palace Saloon or one of his other regular saloons where whiskey seemed to be a natural accompaniment to poker or Faro.

It was late afternoon by the time he arrived back in Tombstone. He took El Rosillo straight to the Dexter Livery Stable on Fremont Street. Old

John Dunbar ran it now and had a real way with horses, which George liked. He had never really cottoned to Dunbar's former partner John Behan, who had been a part-owner until he became first the undersheriff and then sheriff before he left Tombstone for Yuma in 1887. As a friend of the Earps, George didn't care much for the way he had sided with The Cowboys, or for the way that he supplemented his income by siphoning off money from the numerous gambling joints and brothels.

From the livery he walked along a block and dropped into the *Tombstone Epitaph* offices, where he found Stanley Bagg overseeing his hard-working printers, while filling the air with his inevitable cigars.

Stanley beamed when he saw George, before punching a worktop when he saw George's melancholic shake of the head.

"I was too late, Stanley."

"Darn it! I was hoping I'd have good news about your surgical skills two days running." He picked up and handed George a fresh copy of the *Epitaph* from a pile on the floor. "Take that and have a read later on. Now tell me exactly what happened."

George followed him into the editor's office, placed his G. W. Elliott saddlebags on the floor by the desk then sat down and filled and lit his pipe. He told him everything, including details about the operation and Handy's death just as he was closing up the wound. Stanley made rapid notes with the practiced ease of a well-seasoned journalist.

He struck a light to his cigar, immediately provoking a fit of coughing. He noticed George's raised eyebrow.

"I know, you told me off about the cigars. But go on; tell me what's happened to the fellow who shot him? What was his name?"

"Francis J. Heney, a Tucson lawyer. He submitted himself for arrest and there'll be a trial. A long one, I imagine."

Stanley shook his head. "I deal in news, George, as you well know. In my experience, all news sells papers, but I can't say that I ever enjoy making money out of bad news. Handy's death is bad news indeed."

George leaned forward and tapped the ashes out of his pipe. "I've lost the taste for that smoke. It's bad news, all right and I feel bad that I couldn't help him. It was just too long before the cutting started."

"That's not your fault, George. You can't be everywhere."

George stood up. "I know that, but it still rankles, Stanley. He was a colleague. And he was a good doctor, even if he had his faults."

Stanley's eyes enlarged. "Faults, George?"

George smiled for the first time and gripped the

lapels of his coat. Stanley watched his jaw rise and knew what was coming next. He recognized the George Goodfellow mannerism that indicated a burst of pomposity was about to erupt.

He was right.

"Well, I'm afraid that you're going to have to do some digging elsewhere if you want any dirt on the subject," George said. "He was my patient, Stanley, and as you know, I am therefore bound by my Hippocratic Oath. I cannot and will not divulge anything else."

Stanley tossed his pencil on the desk. "Of course, George. I'll write all this up and have it in the next issue."

George grunted and picked up his saddlebags. "Well, I'd better go see Edith and Stella. With any luck they'll have some food. I must say that my stomach is feeling like my throat was cut." He smiled again as he picked up the newspaper and tucked it under his arm. "Like that miner I operated on yesterday, actually. Did you know that he absconded from the hospital before I could tend to his wound. Damned fool pulled his tracheotomy tube out."

Stanley winced. "That must have hurt."

"It would have done. And the damned fool hadn't paid me for saving his life."

"Some folks are just plumb ungrateful, George."

"He sure was. Apparently he left saying that he was going to kill me." He harrumphed as he put on his hat. "I'll be seeing you, Stanley. Maybe some cards and a drink sometime?"

Stanley watched his friend leave the office. He was well aware that George was hurting. It wasn't that he believed he was a saint, as the good folk of Sonora thought and called him. It was just that he hated to lose a patient.

Stella and Edith were baking and after telling them the sad news about Dr. John Handy he sat at the kitchen table and ate a generous portion of apple pie and drank a pot of coffee.

"That is awful, Daddy," said Edith, once George had finished eating. "Why do men have to have guns? They kill people."

George sighed. He was all too well aware that Stella was vehemently against guns, as was his late wife, Katherine. Although he had to deal with their results, he both owned and carried guns when he needed to and he was prepared to use them.

"It is a difficult issue, Edith, my dear. You know about the United States Constitution, don't you?"

"Of course, Daddy," she replied with slightly beetled brows.

"Well, according to the Second Amendment to the United States Constitution, it is every individual's right to keep and bear arms."

Stella was sitting opposite him with her arms

firmly crossed and her lips tightly pressed together. She caught George's forbidding look and said nothing.

But Edith was capable of holding her own in a discussion. Indeed, George had always encouraged that.

"But just because you have a right to do something, that doesn't make it . . . well, doesn't make it right, does it, Daddy?"

George smiled. "No, it doesn't make it right, but unless everyone gave up their right to carry a gun, and I mean everyone, there would be a real danger. The problem is that there are bad people who would still carry guns, so they would be even more dangerous. If people have the right to carry a gun then they can at least defend themselves."

"But I don't suppose Doctor Handy was carrying a gun?"

George saw that the discussion was going to get difficult without explaining some of the background to the affair. That he was not prepared to do, even to win an argument. For one thing, he considered Edith too young to hear about Dr. Handy's domestic problems.

"No, Edith, Doctor Handy was not carrying a gun."

"Then the man who did it must have been a bad man."

"We can't say that, Edith, my dear. You see, he says that he was carrying his gun to defend himself. And he claims that he was defending himself from Doctor Handy."

"Then I don't believe him. I don't think Doctor Handy would attack anyone."

George tousled her hair. "Well, that is not up to us to decide. That is where the law comes in, Edith. There will be a trial and it will all be decided in court."

"Well, I liked Doctor Handy and I am sad about it."

"I know, Edith. I am sad too. I tried to save him."

Edith nodded. "Do you mind if I go and read now?"

"I never mind you reading, my dear. I'll be going out again soon. I have a patient to see."

Once Edith had gone, Stella started to clear the table. She pointed to the *Epitaph.*

"Mister Bagg has written a good piece about you, Doctor Goodfellow, sir. At least you managed to save that miner."

George picked up the newspaper and scanned the article. "Yes, I saved him, Stella."

He didn't want to explain any more about him, especially since the miner had threatened to kill him. Nor, in view of the discussion that he had just had with Edith, did he intend to tell her that as a precaution he had a derringer in his coat pocket as well as his Italian poniard dagger in its concealed sheath.

• • •

Carlton Levine let George in and shook his hand.

"I am sorry that I couldn't come earlier. I was called away to Tucson."

"I know, George. The whole of Tombstone heard about it. Were you able to help?"

"No, I am afraid not. The patient had been shot too many hours before."

Carlton patted George on the shoulder. "Well, if you couldn't help, George, then I am sure that no one could."

George grunted noncommittally. "But more importantly, how is Esme?"

Carlton's face clouded. "Not so well, I am afraid. She is not vomiting as much, but she feels weak and is still having pains."

George followed the schoolteacher through to the bedroom.

Esme was lying back against the pillows. She was stroking a sleek black cat that lay curled up on the bedspread.

"Ah, Doctor Goodfellow. How good of you to come. Carlton told me that you had been called away."

"How are you feeling, Esme?"

"I . . . I am a little better, I think. I have been managing some beef tea that Carlton made me. He always gives me it when I am poorly."

"Good. Beef tea is a good restorative. And perhaps you'll manage some soup tomorrow."

George turned. "I'd like to examine Esme's abdomen again. Could you give us five minutes?"

"Of course, just call me when you are ready."

Once they were alone George waited for Esme to pull down the bedcovers and pull up her nightgown to let him look at her abdomen.

He rubbed his hands, as he habitually did before palpating a patient's abdomen. "Apologies if my hand is cold."

He felt around her tummy, then percussed as he had done the day before, before pulling out his stethoscope to listen.

"Is that any less tender?"

She gave the slightest nod. "A little easier, thank you."

"Which means it feels almost as bad, I think," George stated. "And it feels exactly the same, which is what I would expect." He pulled her nightdress down and replaced the bedcovers. "Have you reconsidered about telling Carlton what I found?"

Esme looked at the cat, which had remained undisturbed throughout the examination. She reached out and stroked behind its ears. In response the cat purred, opened its eyes and licked her hand.

"I know what you want, Tabitha," she said, reaching for a cookie from a box on the bedside table. "You want one of Fiona Parker's cinnamon and arrowroot cookies, don't you?" She laid it in front of the cat, who immediately started licking the cinnamon powder from it before picking it up in its mouth and jumping down from the bed.

"That's a fine cat you have there."

"She's my best friend, Doctor Goodfellow. She loves these cookies that Fiona Parker sends me."

George nodded. He recalled seeing her with conjunctivitis the morning before, after he had operated on Red Douglas, the miner. "Fiona Parker, the librarian. She is also an assistant teacher at Carlton's school, isn't she?"

Esme frowned and George noticed a tightening of her jaw muscles. "That's right. She is so talented—in so many ways." She brushed the powder from her fingers. "But regarding your question, my mind is made up. I don't want Carlton to know."

"Do you mind telling me why not, Esme?"

"It's complicated, Doctor Goodfellow. I . . . I have a lot to think about. Maybe soon I will be able to tell him."

George clicked his tongue and stood up. He opened the door and called Carlton through.

"I think there is a very slight improvement, Carlton. I'd like you to keep giving Esme the same medicine and try to get her onto clear soup tomorrow, if the vomiting doesn't worsen."

"Will you be calling again?" Carlton asked.

"In a few days. I have to go away for a short spell and I'll be taking Edith, my daughter."

"Somewhere nice, I hope?" Esme asked.

"I think she'll like it," George replied as he picked up his medical bag. "She doesn't know about it yet. It's a surprise."

Carlton laughed. "Well, everyone enjoys being surprised."

Esme shook her head. "Not everyone likes surprises, Carlton. I am sure that I don't."

As George walked back to his house he couldn't help but wonder what Esme Levine meant.

# Chapter 6
## THE SNAKE RANCH

Edith had been delighted when George informed her that they were all going to pay a visit to the ranch.

"But I thought you said that we had to wait until your practice became a bit less busy?" Edith asked.

George laughed. "I did, but I just decided that I need a break from medicine and surgery and you my dear daughter need to see those brands on the cattle at the Snake Ranch."

Stella was not quite so enthusiastic. "And I suppose that I had better get my housecleaning things ready? Every time we go there, I find an accumulation of dust and sand in all of the rooms."

"That's what you have to expect in the Huachuca Mountains, Stella."

"And it will be a sticky journey in this heat."

"It will, and we'll have company on the way there," George went on with a grin. "Well, not exactly live company."

Edith wrinkled her nose in disgust. "Daddy, we're not taking some dead creature, are we?"

"In a manner of speaking. We'll be taking a

dead pig. The hands at the ranch will welcome it and I daresay you'll not mind some pork."

"But did you say we were taking a whole pig?" Stella asked in bemusement."

"I did. I ordered it from Godfrey Tribolet, the butcher." His eyes twinkled. "But of course we'll only need so much of it. The rest I'll need for some experiments."

"Experiments, Daddy!" Edith exclaimed with delight. "Can I help you with them?"

George tousled her hair. "Afraid not with these ones, my little princess. These are grown up experiments."

Then seeing her dejected look he smiled. "But I tell you what. While we're there we'll do a little geology and I'll take you out to look for fossils."

"Fossils! That's amazing," Edith gasped. "Can I go and look up one of your books in your study?"

"Of course you can, Princess. You'll find them under—"

"I know! Under G for Geology."

George chuckled and even Stella managed a smile.

"Science," he said simply.

"Just please don't bring back too many old rocks with you, Doctor Goodfellow, sir. They accumulate dust."

The journey early the next day proved perfectly enjoyable for all three of them. George drove the wagon that he had kept from his expedition to the Sonora earthquake disaster and which he had gotten Zach Donoghue, the carpenter to install a comfortable upholstered bench seat behind him, covered by a folding canopy so that Stella and Edith could ride in comfort. In the back was their luggage and various boxes full of books and some scientific paraphernalia for the trip. And under a tarpaulin at the very back was the carcass of the pig that he had collected from Godfrey Tribolet that morning.

Tied to the back and contentedly coming along behind was El Rosillo, saddled and bearing the doctor's G. W. Elliott medical saddlebags.

Every now and then Edith would burst into song and the two adults would join in. George enjoyed himself, but yet he kept a watch on the terrain, just in case they should have any unexpected or unwelcome visitors. Despite their proximity to Fort Huachuca there were still reports of occasional forays by renegade apaches from the San Carlos Reservation.

Despite Stella's dislike of weapons, George was carrying his Navy Colt in the holster that hung by his side, and his Winchester was propped against his seat, within instant reach.

But thankfully, there were no unwanted visitors.

George had bought a share in the Snake Ranch in the Huachuca Mountains, about eight miles from Charleston, on the San Pedro River some years before. It had formerly belonged to the Huachuca Cattle Company until George bought it with Joe Brown, whose store in Tombstone stocked everything from every type of musical instrument, to paint, brushes or even a baby buggy. The ranch consisted of well over two hundred fenced acres that supported a herd of longhorns and a ranch crew of half a dozen hands, a cook and a foreman.

The ranch house was comfortable, but fairly spartanly furnished. Although Joe Brown was part owner, he rarely visited, so the study overlooking the range was effectively George's preserve. It had well-stocked bookcases, a huge map of the area pinned to a wall, a large desk littered with business papers and ledgers, a tobacco jar and rack of pipes, a large magnifying glass on a mounted rotating arm and a microscope.

Dan Legg, the foreman, a competent man of about forty with a huge handlebar mustache, helped George unload the wagon while Stella went from room to room checking on what jobs needed doing about the ranch house. That left Edith to enjoy herself darting back and forth soaking up the atmosphere of the ranch. First, she went down to the bunkhouse to talk with Hector MacLeod, the ever-cheerful old Scottish cook, to tell him that her father had brought a whole pig, and then she went to watch the horses in the corral.

Hector followed her. "Don't go too close to that roan, my wee hen," he cautioned. "He's a biter. He took a piece out of young Hank's behind the other day. We thought we would have to take him in to Tombstone to see the doctor."

He produced a corncob pipe and struck a light to it. "Fortunately, the bleeding stopped when we told him that Doctor Goodfellow would have to stitch him up."

Edith's eyes widened in amazement. "Did it really stop bleeding just because he was scared?"

"It did. Fear can be a great medicine, you see, my wee hen."

George came down from the ranch house and crossed the yard to join them.

"Your daughter tells me we'll be having pork, Doctor Goodfellow," Hector said, gleefully rubbing his hands. "A whole pig! The boys will like that and I can't wait to get cooking pork for a change."

George raised an eyebrow at Edith. "Actually, it is not the whole pig, Hector, but you can have some of it."

"Some of it?" Hector repeated, his jolly round face showing his bemusement.

"That's right. I need most of it you see, and after I've used it I fear it won't be fit for human consumption."

Hector took off his hat and scratched his bald

head. "Sounds a waste of good food to me, Doctor, but you are the boss."

"That's what I thought," George said with a twinkle of amusement. "So go and get your butchery instruments and come over to the wagon. I'll show you which parts you can take."

Hector watched him walk off and then smiled at Edith. "Is your father feeling all right, my wee hen? He's not been working too hard, has he?"

"Daddy always works too hard," she replied with a grin. "But he's not going to eat it all himself. It will be for an experiment."

Understanding dawned on Hector. "Of course. The doctor and his science. That makes it as clear as mud to me, but at least the boys are getting some pork."

With which he scuttled off to get his butchery equipment.

Later that afternoon George and Edith rode out with Dan Legg to see the boys do some branding. George had told Dan that Edith was excited to see her brand being used, so Dan had arranged for three of the hands to work the north stretch along the banks of the San Pedro.

"It is an honor having you with us, Miss Edith," Dan said with a tip of his hat. "I've got the boys to show you how we rope and brand them."

Edith smiled and blushed. "That makes me feel very special, Mister Legg."

"And special you are, Miss Edith. There aren't too many young ladies who have their very own cattle brand."

Up ahead they spotted the men working in the scrub near the river bank. They rode up and stopped to watch the two mounted hands, and smelled the smoke of the fire where a third hand was taking the roped young calves and branding them with a hot iron.

The three men worked as a team, two without leaving their saddles, the other on foot. One of the riders would chase a beast out of the scrub, then rope its head, drag it towards the fire so that it turned, while the other snared its pirouetting hind legs. Then the head roper, a lanky individual wearing a battered old Stetson, whistled. Upon this signal his comrade, a stocky bareheaded youngster, backed up. In a moment the calf was stretched out, ready for the third hand, a cowhand with prodigious bowlegs, to leap forward to give the beast its hot tattoo.

"We're branding all the free calves, Dan explained to Edith. Ordinarily we'd do them in the spring, but the doctor thought it would be good for you to see just how it is done."

"Howdy, Miss Edith," said the cowboy with the brand. "This the first time you've seen branding? Hope it hasn't upset you none."

"Hello Mister Bendy," Edith replied. "No it doesn't upset me. My Daddy is a doctor and I've seen patients with far worse things than a brand. I think it looks pretty. GEG. That's Edith inside Daddy's initials of G.G. He told me that, even though the E could stand for Emory, his middle name."

The three hands had all chuckled at Edith's use of his name, for "Bendy" was typical southwestern humor, referring to his bowlegs, a result of a lifetime of riding and cattle punching.

"Glad you like it, Miss Edith," Bendy replied, releasing the calf to dash off into the scrub.

George dismounted and strode over to the fire. He shoved his hands in his pockets and toed one of the branding irons. "Have we had any trouble with cattle going missing, boys?"

"Not this past year, Doctor Goodfellow," Dan replied, leaning on his saddle horn. "We did have some Apaches stealing a couple or so back then, but what with the fencing and us all keeping a good watch out, no sir, we've had no problems at all. And I guess that with Fort Huachuca being not too far away, we are not as troubled as the old Huachuca Cattle Company would have been."

George took a deep sniff through his nose. "I love the air here in the Huachuca Mountains." He pointed towards pinewoods in the distance. "I'm going to be going over there tomorrow afternoon, Dan. I'll need to be on my own, so tell the rest of the boys to stay clear, will you?"

"I will do, Doctor Goodfellow."

"I'll need to take my wagon. And don't any of you worry if you hear shooting. There's no reason to hightail it over. It'll be me."

"Practicing shooting or hunting, Doctor Goodfellow?" Bendy asked.

"Nope! Neither of those. Just need to be by myself," George said cryptically, as he returned to his horse and mounted up. "Come on Dan, let's take Edith on a proper look around."

And without another word he set off.

Dan knew better than to ask what George was up to himself. Hector MacLeod had told him that George had been acting cagey with him.

"It will be an experiment," Edith whispered to the foreman.

"Ah, I see," Dan whispered back. "I'm sure your father knows what he's doing."

"He usually does," Edith replied. "Especially about experiments and science. He's going to take me fossil collecting tomorrow afternoon."

"And what would fossils be, Miss Edith. You'll excuse me, but I didn't have anywhere near as much learning as your father did."

"Animals and bugs and creatures that are so old they've turned into stone."

"Stone critters," Dan said in amazement. Then he laughed. "Old Hector is pretty old. I guess I had better warn him he needs to move about a bit more instead of sitting around in that kitchen, or he'll turn into stone some day."

Edith started to giggle and Dan joined in.

"What are you two laughing about?" George asked, turning around in the saddle and grinning at them. "Nothing at my expense I hope."

"No sir," replied Dan, winking at Edith. "Miss Edith was just telling me about the stone critters you're going to show her. I was just wondering if they was what you were going to be shooting at? The thing is, maybe you won't bring any of them down, because bullets just bounce off of stone."

They all caught the laughing habit right then.

Hector cooked up a great meal of roast pork for all of the hands, who ate it in the bunkhouse as usual. He prepared a separate meal in the ranch house for George, Stella, Edith and Dan.

"I wish we came out here more often, Hector," Stella said at the end of the meal when Hector came to clear everything away. "I cannot tell you how pleasant it is to have someone cook for me. And you have a way with food."

"He does indeed, ma'am," Dan agreed. That's the main reason that the boys at the Snake Ranch are so happy to keep working up here."

"That and the fact that they are well paid," put in George.

"That as well, Doctor Goodfellow," said Hector, with plates and pots stacked on his tray.

"But as a doctor I am sure that you agree that the way to a man's heart is through his stomach."

George gave a slight shrug of the shoulders. "Well, the two organs are in fairly close proximity, the heart lying above the stomach, but the two are of course separated by the diaphragm. Now if you mean could . . ."

"Oh Daddy, you know what Mister Hector means!" exclaimed Edith with a squeal of amusement.

George gave a short laugh. "I know, Princess. He is talking metaphorically and I totally agree." He gave his stomach a pat. "I for one have an entirely satisfied stomach and heart after that delicious pork."

"And I'll be back with coffee and apple pie," Hector beamed as he backed through the door. "And milk for Miss Edith."

"Seriously though, Doctor Goodfellow," Dan said after he had gone. "Hector MacLeod's cooking gives the boys something to look forward to every day. A good breakfast and a good dinner to look forward to will keep a cowboy grinning all day despite any amount of saddle sore or aching muscles. That and a good game of cards in the evening after he's eaten."

George laughed. "A good game of cards goes down well with most folks. I enjoy a few hands at the Crystal Palace Saloon myself."

Dan laughed. "But we don't play for high

stakes here, sir. I don't allow that. If one hand started taking the other's hard earned money it would be a recipe for bad feeling, and we know how that could end up, don't we, sir?"

"I do indeed, Dan. So I thank you. The last thing I'd want would be to have to come out here to treat a gunshot wound."

"It will never happen, sir. All I let the boys play for is matchsticks. They imagine it is money and get a kick out of that. Then Hector lets them use their matchstick money to buy cookies."

Stella laughed. "Good old Hector. It seems he is right in what he says, Doctor Goodfellow, sir. "He gets straight to the men's hearts through their stomachs."

They were still laughing when Hector returned with apple pie, a pot of coffee and milk for Edith.

But though he was outwardly laughing, George's mind was elsewhere. He was thinking of how many times he had performed autopsy examinations of men killed in shootings. And on at least two occasions a bullet had passed through the stomach and then through the heart.

Both had been in saloon shootings when a man had been challenged at a card table and shot from underneath the table.

"Can we play cards later, Daddy?" Edith asked.

That broke his train of thought. He smiled and patted her hand. "Of course, my dear."

"Stella, too. And can we play for cookies?"

"Cookies?" Hector asked. "Would you like me to bring some over, Doctor? I have a batch freshly baked."

Stella gave George a disapproving look. "I am not sure that teaching Edith to gamble would be very suitable."

George frowned, but he had to agree.

"We'll just play for fun, Princess."

Hector grinned. "But don't worry, Miss Edith, I'll bring over the cookies anyway."

George found it hard to get to sleep that night, since he could not get the image of Dr. John Handy from his mind. Accordingly, he went through to his study and by the light of his desk lamp, poured a large whiskey and charged his pipe from the tobacco jar as he sat behind his desk to look through some of the papers and books he had brought with him from Tombstone.

Topmost was a copy of the *Southern California Practitioner*, from March 1887. He opened it to page 95.

Notes on the Impenetrability of Silk to Bullets
By G. E. Goodfellow, MD.,
Tombstone, Arizona.

It was a relatively short article that he had written and which he thought would be one of those little curios that might pique the interest of his fellow physicians and surgeons. It certainly had, the result being numerous invitations from various medical societies for him to go and lecture.

He settled back, his pipe clenched between his teeth and read.

> A somewhat extensive experience in the gunshot wounds of civil life, during the past few years, has brought to my attention the following instances illustrative of the remarkable tenacity of silk fiber and its resistance power of a bullet:

He smiled as he read, for he always found reading his own words to be a strange experience, since he used the tone that he would use to deliver a lecture to his colleagues. He imagined that some would consider him a tad bombastic.

Then as he read on he remembered the three cases as if they had occurred only days before.

> In the spring of 1881 I was a few feet distant from a couple of individuals who were quarreling. They began shooting. The first shot took effect, as was afterwards ascertained, in the left breast of one of them, who, after being shot, and while staggering back some twelve feet, cocked and fired his pistol twice, his second shot

going into the air, for by that time he was on his back. He never made a motion after pulling the trigger the second time, the pistol dropping to the ground with his hands.

He puffed his pipe and pictured the scene. It could almost have been the sort of sensational stuff that people like Ned Buntline would use in their dime novels. But of course, apart from a need to be scientifically rigorous, he had to maintain the confidentiality of the case, according to his Hippocratic Oath, so he wrote the simple bare facts.

He recalled it so well. Luke Short was a professional gambler who was at that time the Faro dealer at the Oriental Saloon. He was a real dandy who was fastidious in his dress, always sporting a tailored suit and more often than not, wore a top hat and silver topped cane. At a mere five-foot-six he looked relatively innocuous, which was the complete opposite of what he really was. His right pants pocket was tailored especially long and lined with leather to contain his six-gun. His unfortunate opponent was a gunfighter called Charlie Storms who had lost his temper over a game and threatened him.

Bat Masterton, one of Wyatt Earp's friends was also working as a house dealer and he intervened and defused the situation, albeit only temporarily.

Later that day, Storms pulled Short off the sidewalk and went for his gun. George happened to be on the street at the time and saw the whole thing. It was to be Storm's last mistake, for Luke Short was the faster and he fired twice. Storms was dead before he hit the ground.

George read on.

> Half an hour afterward I made an examination of the body. Upon stripping it, found not a drop of blood had come from either of the two wounds received. From the wound in his left breast a silk handkerchief protruded, which I presumed had been stuffed in by some of his friends to prevent bleeding. I withdrew it and with it came the bullet. It was then seen that it had been carried in by the ball.

He took a sip of whiskey as he read and recalled the autopsy.

> Upon opening the body, the track of the ball was found to be as follows: through the left ventricle, thence through the descending aorta; thence into and through the body of either the second or third dorsal vertebra into the spinal canal, fracturing the lamina. The ball came from a cut-off Colt .45 caliber revolver, fired

> at a distance of six feet, the cartridge of which contains thirty grains of powder and two hundred and sixty grains of lead. The man had on a light summer suit, the handkerchief being in the breast pocket of the coat.
> Examination of the handkerchief showed only two slight tears or cuts in it, they being on the outside of the fold containing the bullet, where it had struck the bones of the vertebral column, no ribs having been touched. There were two thicknesses of silk covering the bullet.
> This attracted my attention, but in a short time a still more remarkable case was observed.

George drained his whiskey and poured another as he read his report of the second shooting.

> During a fight a man was wounded at a distance of thirty feet by a load from a shotgun. The cartridge contained four drams of powder and twelve buckshot. Four of the buckshot penetrated the frontal bone, and, as shown by the autopsy, flattening themselves against the posterior wall of the skull; more entered the face, piercing the facial bones, and some passed through the upper thoracic

wall, thence into the lungs. At the same time he was shot he had loosely tied about his neck a red silk Chinese handkerchief. In the folds of this I found two buckshot, neither of which had so much as cut a fiber of the silk. There were four or six folds of the silk between the balls and the skin. The uncertainty as to the number of layers arises from the fact that not wishing to damage the specimen, I never unfolded the handkerchief to ascertain exactly.

He swirled the whiskey in his glass as he pictured the gunshot man involved. In fact, once again the story had been more complex than his medical paper had needed; hence he had stuck to the salient medical and forensic details. The death had been the result of a shootout at the Chandler Ranch a few miles out of town. Deputy Sheriff Billy Breakenridge had led a posse to surprise and apprehend a couple of rustlers by the names of Zwing Hunt and Billy Grounds. The ensuing gunfight left John Gillespie, one of the possemen dead and two other possemen wounded. Zwing Hunt was shot through the chest, but survived. Billy Grounds, the other rustler took a charge of buckshot full in the face, from Billy Breakenridge.

News of the shootout reached Tombstone and

Police Chief Dave Neagle got hold of George and together they rode out in an ambulance. It took George several hours patching up the living. Among them was Billy Grounds, but he didn't last too many hours.

To fully appreciate this case, it is necessary to understand that the shot which went into the forehead passed through a thick Mexican white felt hat weighing, untrimmed, twelve ounces, heavily embroidered with silver, and a silver wire snake an inch thick for a band. The thickness and weight of these hats can only be realized by those who have seen and worn them. Two of the balls penetrated the band, then entered the skull. The shots entering the chest, one of which went through the sternum into the depths of the chest, had to pass through two heavy wool shirts and a blanket-lined canvas coat and vest, such as are worn in the West. A few layers of light silk, however, were enough to stop bullets that could pass through all the tissues mentioned.

His pipe had gone cold so he tapped out the ashes and the dottle and refilled it. When he had lit it to his satisfaction he read on:

The third case was that of a man wounded at a distance not exceeding three feet, by a ball from a full-length .45 caliber Colt revolver. The ball entered the right side of the neck two inches below the angle of the jaw at the posterior border of the sterno-cleido-mastoid muscle and emerged on the left side at the angle of the jaw. The head was turned slightly to the right at the time the bullet struck him. Around his neck was loosely tied a red silk handkerchief, as in the preceding case. The ball catching this carried a portion of it through to the wound, then slipped off, leaving the handkerchief in the wound uncut. This man recovered, though the carotid artery of the right side could be felt bared and pulsating in the wound.

He subsequently told me, for I never saw him to speak to but twice, that all the liquids he took passed out of the wound of entrance for some weeks. He is now, I presume, pursuing his trade (cattle-stealing) on the border—if not in peace, at least in prosperity.

The life of this man was, presumably, saved by the handkerchief; for had it not been dragged into the wound I doubt not that the great vessels of the right side would have been irreparably injured.

The ball that killed the first man, above mentioned, fired from the distance at which he was shot, ordinarily goes through the body, bones or no bones, as I have seen illustrated many times. Fired into a four-inch plank of pine or redwood it readily passed through, and sinks into another a foot behind. At fourteen feet the same caliber ball penetrated a six-inch pine joist, and struck the ground some twenty feet beyond, with force to flatten the ball. No experiments have been made with the shotgun; but in two cases, now called to mind, where the distance was greater and the charge of the powder less by one dram. In one case, at a distance of 120 feet, the humerus and one of the lumbar vertebral spinous processes were fractured, the balls passing respectively through an overcoat and two shirts, and the same with the addition of the waistband of the trousers. In the other, with the same charge of powder, at a distance of sixty feet, one of the shots entered the head of the tibia, some two inches below the knee joint, passed through and buried itself in the lower end of the femur an inch: this, after piercing leather boot-top, canvas overall and drawers. Had the handkerchief not been in the way in the first case, the bullet would have gone entirely through the body. The second case is the test. Balls propelled from the same barrels, and by the same amount of powder, penetrated the tissues described, yet failed to go through four or six folds of thin silk.

George sat back and tapped the paper with his fingers. He had always meant to follow up on the paper with another one. He smiled to himself as he laid his pipe in the ashtray and placed the journal in a paper basket on the corner of the desk.

"We shall see," he said to himself as he stood up. "But first thing in the morning, it will be time to show Edith a little of the wonders of the earth."

# Chapter 7
# FOSSILS AND EXPERIMENTS

After a good breakfast George and Edith rode out towards the mountains to the west. Edith had learned to ride when she was about four years old and loved the little cowpony that George kept at the Snake Ranch for her. In his saddlebags he had hammers, and a map that he had drawn himself after he had surveyed the area when he first bought the ranch. Teaching her about geography and geology while having fun was his idea of education.

And she absorbed it all with alacrity, for spending time with her father, now that her mother had died, was in her mind the best thing one could do.

"Will it be far, Daddy?"

"Just to the edge of the mountains, then we'll need to scramble up into the hills. That's why you're wearing those range clothes. We don't want to get those precious little knees of yours grazed on rocks or cactus, do we?"

"And will we really find fossils, Daddy?"

"We will indeed. I know just the place."

He grinned at her as she beamed with pleasure and enthusiasm.

It took them about half an hour to reach the foothills which were covered in a mix of oak, ponderosa and Apache pines with thickets of whitethorn scrub. They tethered their mounts and George pulled off his saddlebag and drew out a map.

"You see where we're heading, Princess," he said, tracing a route up the hills. "Each of these contour lines represent—"

"Different altitudes. I know, Daddy. I'm not a little girl."

"George laughed as he folded the map away and then with the saddlebags over his shoulder he led the way up through the trees.

"Keep a close watch and you should see lots of different birds up here, Edith. We've got hummingbirds, tyrant flycatchers and if you're lucky, maybe a red crossbill or two."

"I love all the different types of butterflies," Edith enthused.

"Yes, this is God's land, Princess. You'll find many of his wonderful creatures up here."

"It's so beautiful, Daddy. Just like the Garden of Eden."

George smiled ruefully as he kept on walking upwards. He knew that her mother had liked to inculcate her own beliefs into his daughter. As a man with a scientific leaning he wanted to use the trip to give her more of an understanding about evolution. He planned to do it slowly, letting her absorb the things he was going to teach her about Charles Darwin and his theory of evolution. In his library in Tombstone he had a copy of Darwin's *On the Origin of Species*, as well as Alfred Russel Wallace's book, *Contributions to the Theory of Natural Selection*.

He felt that both scientists had pushed back the frontiers of knowledge and understanding to arrive at a theory of evolution, albeit coming at it from different directions. Darwin had postulated that it was all about the survival of the fittest, whereas Wallace considered that creatures evolved by adapting to their geographical home.

He was aware that many scientists were proposing that God did not exist, but as a believer himself he saw no incompatibility between belief in the Lord and a belief in evolution. To his mind evolution was merely the way that God allowed creatures to develop. He just wanted to open Edith's mind up to such possibilities, hence the geography and geology trip that they were on.

"If you look over to the east you'll see that the stone is very different from here," he said once they reached a plateau and he set down his saddlebags and drew out a couple of small handpick hammers. "That is Precambrian granite. Over here the rock is predominantly Cretaceous sediment. Effectively, you will find no fossils over in the granite, because it is so old that it is older than life itself. On the other hand, the

Cretaceous is much younger and we should find lots of early fossils."

And he showed her how to use her pick hammer to chip rock and split stones.

"These are fossilized worms," he said, handing a rock with the distinct cylindrical outlines of a couple of worms."

After an hour they had collected some trilobites, an ammonite and a near perfectly formed fossil of a beetle.

"Have a look at them all under the magnifying glass, Edith," he said once they had a small collection on the ground in front of them. "And then to be scientific, we need to draw them, add a map of where exactly we found them and describe each one with the date and time of the find. I've brought a notebook and pencils in my saddlebag."

Edith set to with pleasure while George smoked his pipe and arranged a small picnic.

Once Edith had finished drawing the fossils and making a small map, then writing some notes about them they sat and enjoyed their picnic.

"I wish we could find the skeleton of a really big animal," Edith said at last. "Little things are interesting, but big things are better."

George laughed. "Not always, Princess. In science it is sometimes the very small things that matter most. The world that you can see under a microscope is often where the great discoveries are to be made. That is what clever scientists like Louis Pasteur and Robert Koch have discovered. There are little creatures that we call germs that cause all sorts of disease. And you would be surprised at what you can see down a microscope."

He swatted an insect that had been honing in on him as he ate. Then with a laugh he leaned over and drew out a brass field microscope that he always kept with him.

"Look, let's have a look at this little creature." He put the insect on a glass slide then slid it under the lens of the microscope and adjusted first the mirror to illuminate it and then the focus to see the insect's head.

Edith peered down through the lens. "Goodness, Daddy, it has the most huge eyes."

"That's right, dear. In comparison to the size of its head and its brain, the eyes are colossal. They can see in almost all directions, which is why it is so difficult to catch one—unless you are as fast as me!"

Edith laughed. "Why did you become a doctor instead of a teacher, Daddy? You are so good at it. I think you'd be as good a teacher as you are a doctor."

George felt that familiar pang of guilt. At the moment he was going through one of the inevitable periods of self-doubt about his doctoring skills. He hadn't been able to save his friend Doctor John Handy, or do anything for Katherine, his own wife.

"I don't know, Princess, life doesn't always turn out the way you expect it to. All in all I think I am probably more use as a doctor than I would be as a teacher."

"When can I go back to school, Daddy? I miss my friends and I think they would stop me thinking about Mama." Her eyes welled up and George reached out and drew her to him.

"I understand, Princess. I miss your mama, too." He hugged her reassuringly and let her weep. But her tears did not last long, for she had a toughness that was undoubtedly inherited from George's side of the family.

"Couldn't I go to school here in Tombstone for a while? Carrie Bagg goes and we are really good friends."

George stroked her head. "I'll see what I can do, Princess."

They returned to the ranch house by mid afternoon, where George left Edith to bombard Stella with information about fossils and geology as she showed her the fossil collection and her drawings.

Dan Legg had arranged everything according to George's instructions and so, after collecting his Navy Colt and his Winchester rifle, some ammunition and a carpetbag that he had brought from Tombstone, George drove towards the distant pinewoods where he knew he would be alone and left undisturbed. Dan had thought it odd that his employed had wanted the pig carcass loaded onto the wagon again, yet he knew better than to question him. It was good enough for him to know that he was "experimenting."

Twenty minutes later George jumped down from the wagon and lifted out the pig carcass. He carried it over to the base of a tall pine and propped it against it. Then he brought the bag over and from it pulled out a number of his wife's old silk blouses.

"I know that you wouldn't mind me using these, Katherine," he said, closing his eyes for a moment. "This is in the cause of science."

He dressed the carcass in two blouses, one on top of the other, then added a third, but only on one side, letting the other half hang down behind it. Finally, he draped another over its head.

He took out a notebook and jotted down details about the date and time. Then he wrote:

    Head—single layer
    Right side—two layers
    Left side—three layers

He went back to the wagon and took out the Winchester and laid it against the wheel while he strapped on his gun belt and Navy Colt.

Then from the pig carcass he paced out respectively, thirty, sixty and 120 feet.

The wind had been changing and he cursed as he felt the pattering of gentle rain.

"Well, I guess Edith and I were lucky this morning. After all, Huachuca means 'place of thunder.' If it gets up and starts thundering it will tone down the noise I'm about to make."

And starting at the most distant mark, he began firing with his Winchester. He aimed carefully and shot at the head, then at the right side and the left side of the torso, firing a shot at both chest and abdomen.

And as he suspected it would, the thunder started to peel out, followed by an occasional flash of lightning.

He ignored it, for in a way he had always found thunder and lightning somewhat exhilarating. He moved forward and fired his Colt at the same targets, from sixty and then thirty feet.

"Well, let's see the damage." He drew out a small wooden case containing some surgical instruments.

As he expected the rifle bullets made the most mess. The shot to the head blew a hole straight through the blouse and through the whole head, yet even then, when he withdrew the bullet with a pair of forceps from the tree trunk behind, he found that it was covered in a remnant of silk. The shot to the right side of the torso had penetrated to the chest cavity, but had not ripped the blouse. The three layers on the left side were still intact, although the bullet had lodged in the thick muscle.

Then he compared the bullets from the Colt.

"Pig tissue is pretty similar to human flesh," he mused to himself. "And the shots from the Colt speak for themselves. With three layers it would hurt like hell, but a man would have a good chance of not receiving a fatal wound."

The rain stopped as rapidly as it had started, making his job of extracting bullets easier.

Then he drew a diagram of the pig with a grid next to it. He filled in all the details.

"There is definitely something worth following up on here. It will take more work, but I believe that a vest that is proof against bullets is possible. Maybe have two or three layers with a leather layer inside, like those quilted gambesons that soldiers and knights wore in medieval days. It would certainly make my life as a surgeon in these parts a bit easier."

He then methodically checked each bullet wound and counted each bullet, just as he would do with surgical instruments, swabs or sutures during an operation in case he left something inside a wound.

He was surprised to find that there was one more bullet hole than he expected. It had gone straight through the pig's throat, clearly having struck where he had left the neck exposed. He dug it out of the trachea.

Suddenly, he had the feeling that he was not entirely alone. He spun around, and ducked low, his Navy Colt in his hand at the ready.

But there was no one there.

# Chapter 8
## ANY KIND OF GAME

The next day George left Edith and Stella to amuse themselves at the Snake Ranch and headed off to check on his interests in the Providencia Gold Mine. He employed three miners there, all good experienced men who took pride in their work. He made the trip at least twice a year, in order to show his interest and to make sure that he wasn't just throwing money at a useless venture.

Mining was in George's blood, for his father had often taken him as a youngster to see the various mines that he was responsible for. By the age of ten he knew and could identify all of the different types of ore for gold, silver and lead.

It was fortunate that he had chosen that very time to visit the mine, for the three men were all ill.

"Sorry we ain't working, Doc," said Sam Page, the oldest of the three, a bushy-bearded veteran of half a dozen minefields and the nominal mine boss. "All three of us have had bellyache and the runs for two days."

"And I've been as sick as a dog that ate its own

tail," volunteered Ed Zimmerman, an equally hirsute man of about George's age.

"I only stopped being sick this morning, sir," said Flynn O'Brien, the youngest of the three and the only one who sported a mustache without a beard. "I reckon we'll not be eating any more Rattler stew."

All three were in their own beds in three corners of the cabin they shared. The other corner was taken up with a pot-bellied stove and their table and chairs.

George examined them in turn, washing his hands each time. "You have all still got gurgling abdomens. What makes you think it was rattlesnake stew that did it?"

Sam scratched his beard. "It started the night that we ate it."

"Have you had it before?"

"Sure we have, sir," said Flynn. "Whenever we can catch one we give it a go. We'll give just about any creature a try."

"The thing is that it was tasty," Ed added. "Have you ever had it, Doctor?"

"I have," George replied. "I like it with onions and lots of thyme. Tastes like fishy chicken."

Ed's eyes rolled and he clutched his stomach. "Gah! I still feel sick thinking about it, Doctor."

"Although," George went on, "roast rattlesnake with garlic is my favorite way. Curiously, that seems to taste more like game."

Ed clapped a hand over his mouth, shot out of bed and charged out towards the distant privy.

George grinned. "I'm going to leave you all a bottle of kaolin and morphine to settle your stomachs and stop the runs. I'll also leave a bottle of bismuth for Ed to stop his vomiting."

"You are a gentleman, Doc," said Sam. "I am sorry that none of us are able to show you around the mine this time."

"I'll have a look by myself. How is it going?"

"It is going well, Doc."

"Well enough to keep paying you all?" George said with a smile as he prepared the bottles of medicine from his G. W. Elliott medical saddlebags.

"Ha! And enough to keep turning you a healthy profit, sir," chipped in the ever good humored Flynn.

"Except not so healthy this time, eh?"

"Maybe it was the rattler that wasn't too well, sir?"

Ed returned, his face ashen. With a nod at George he dived back under his blankets.

"On another matter," George went on. "Have any of you seen Red Douglas?"

"Ah, we heard about the fracas you had with him, Doc," said Sam. "He came back, had a fight with one of the Polish miners and almost killed him. Knocked him out."

"Why?"

"He was cross because Jarek Majewski was making fun at him. He was whistling while he talked," said Flynn. "It was a good imitation of how the big Scot sounds now. Did you really make that hole in his throat, Doctor Goodfellow, sir?"

"I did and it saved his life."

Sam shook his head. "That isn't how he sees it, Doc. He was shouting around the camp that he was going to get even with you sometime."

"Is he about?"

Flynn shook his head. "After he knocked Jarek out he gathered his stuff and lit out of the place."

George nodded. The image of the pig carcass with the slug in its throat immediately presented itself to him. During the thunder it was just possible that an extra shot had actually been fired. Maybe he had bent down at the moment it was fired. Maybe he was lucky not to have received a bullet through his own neck. And even if he had been wearing a silk bandana, he knew that wouldn't have saved him.

"Anything wrong, Doc?" Sam asked. "You look like you just saw a ghost."

George gave a short laugh. He realized he was probably just letting his imagination run away with itself. "No boys, there's nothing wrong. Everything is just fine."

• • •

George was pleased to get back to Tombstone and resume his practice. He was particularly pleased to see that Edith had enjoyed herself and been enthused by their fossil hunting. She had occupied herself when he was visiting the mine by making further sketches of plants, grubs and insects viewed through George's magnifying glass.

Although Dr. Henry Matthews had covered his practice while he was away, people having being directed to the other physician's office by a notice pinned under his shingle, judging by the crowd in his waiting room when he opened his afternoon surgery, many patients had preferred to wait for him to return.

First in to see him was the well known China Mary, a rotund Chinese lady who ran a labor agency that supplied Chinese workers to do virtually any kind of manual laboring job, from housekeeping to hefting ore onto wagons, removing dead horses or clearing privies. She ran several laundries, a general store and a restaurant and gambling hall.

She was a pretty, rotund lady who always wore traditional Chinese dress.

"I need your help, Doctor. The usual trouble."

Which meant she needed help with her hemorrhoids and constipation. George felt flattered that she came to him with it rather than seeing one of the handful of Chinese doctors who offered traditional Chinese medicine. She found his rectal ointment and enemas more effective and less unpleasant.

After her he saw a couple of doves from one of the bordellos for some of the intimate problems that they accepted as an occupational risk. And he also saw several men who had male problems that had likely been the result of visiting the same bordellos.

Mrs. Fiona Parker the librarian returned to see him with her conjunctivitis. She was a handsome woman in her late twenties, dressed conservatively as suited a librarian and part time teacher. She had corn-yellow hair, coral blue eyes and full lips. She was a widow of two years; her husband had died from gastro-enteritis during a particularly virulent epidemic in Tombstone.

Her eyes still looked bloodshot.

"I am afraid that the borax eyewash that you gave me the other day hasn't helped at all, Doctor."

George nodded and picked up his Helmholtz ophthalmoscope, an instrument consisting of a handle with a lens and an attached angle mirror. He adjusted the mirror to reflect the sunlight onto the eye, which he then looked at through the lens.

"Hmm, the pupils are working well, so there is no inflammation inside the eyes. This is definitely just a case of conjunctivitis, Missus Parker."

"Can you give me anything else to help it?"

George went over to his medicine cabinet and took out a small ointment container. "I have an excellent remedy here. It is an eye ointment of my own invention consisting of one part citron and four parts spermaceti. I'd like you to smear a little on each eyelid three times a day. And keep using the borax eyewash night and morning."

"And is there anything you can give me for being so tired?"

George smiled. "And what is making you feel so tired? The library or the school?"

She smiled demurely. "A bit of both, I think. But I love both jobs. I love books and I enjoy imparting what little knowledge I have to the children."

"Well, you are not anemic, Missus Parker. I suggest that you try some beef tea. Have it twice a day."

She nodded. "Of course! I should have thought of that myself. Missus Beeton herself recommends that!"

"Missus Beeton? I don't think I know the lady."

She laughed. "Oh, I meant *Mrs. Beeton's Book of Household Management*. It is a book, the very best book ever written in my opinion. I use it to teach the children, especially the girls."

"I shall have to ask my housekeeper about it. I am sure she will have heard about it."

"Oh please do. And if she would like a copy I can put one aside at the library for her."

Once she had gone George washed his hands and reflected about the irony of the different lives of some of his patients. Some of the doves he had seen were intelligent and talented women. Some were entertainers who through circumstance had been forced to sell their feminine charms simply in order to buy food. On the other hand there was Fiona Parker, enjoying her work in the library and school. They seemed worlds apart, yet the fact was that the bordellos had to be licensed to stay open and operate. Those license fees went a long way in paying for both the library and the Tombstone school.

Stanley C. Bagg was next in, along with his daughter Carrie.

Like her father, Carrie was small for her age. She was eleven years old, just like Edith, and like Stanley she also had weak eyesight and had to wear spectacles. But she was one of the most cheerful little girls he ever knew and had a perpetual smile that lifted your spirits just to see her.

"Carrie has a sore throat, George."

"It hurts when I swallow, Doctor Goodfellow," Carrie volunteered. "It feels like it is burning."

George smiled at her and inspected her throat with a throat mirror and a tongue depressor. Then he felt her neck for swollen glands.

"No pus present and no gland swelling. It will be fine in a few days."

He went to his cabinet and dished a few Coltsfoot lozenges into a box. He handed them to Stanley. "I want you to suck one of these four times a day, Carrie. They will soothe that burning feeling."

"That's a relief, George," Stanley said. "I always get a bit nervous when she gets sore throats. Just in case, you know."

George knew only too well. A couple of years back the six-year-old son of one Stanley's printers had developed a sore throat, which had proved to be diphtheria. He had died two days later and his distraught mother had sunk into melancholy and effectively starved herself to death.

George had not been the family doctor and he had been alarmed to hear that the doctor concerned had delayed doing a tracheotomy, which would probably have saved him, but instead went on treating him with hot fomentations to the throat and some sort of cough elixir. When Stanley asked George's opinion about the care given he had declined to directly criticize another doctor, but had merely stated that he would have operated. Stanley had understood what George meant and wrote a scathing article in the *Tombstone Prospector*, the end result being that the said doctor's practice dwindled to nothing and he left, as Stanley said in a later article, to start his malpractice in some other unfortunate town.

"Edith and I were talking about you Carrie," George went on as he sat and made a note of his treatment on a record card. "She wants to come to your school until she goes back East."

Carrie's face burst into a wide grin. "Oh goodie, goodie! We can have such fun."

"Of course, I will have to have a word with Mister Levine, the head teacher first."

"All sounds excellent, George," Stanley said. "Why not ask him tonight at the Schieffelin Hall? There's a theater group doing a Medley of Shakespeare Scenes tonight. I know he'll be going and I thought you were too."

"It slipped my mind, Stanley. I've been a bit pre-occupied. Maybe Carlton won't be there either."

"Because of his wife, Esme? I understand she's been poorly lately."

"She has and I'll be seeing her tomorrow." He nodded pensively. "Shakespeare, eh? I guess I'll see you at the Schieffelin Hall tonight then."

Stanley smiled. "And maybe we'll go to the Oriental Saloon afterwards. There's due to be an arm wrestling competition later tonight, if you remember? I'm sure Carlton will be there if he can."

"Of course. I forgot about the arm wrestling."

Stanley laughed. "Goodness, something really has been eating at your memory, George. How can you forget? It was you, after all who initiated these competitions."

George smiled at Carrie who had started to giggle. "Your father is right, Carrie. In my younger days I did enjoy physical competition."

"You did. Not only did you start these arm-wrestling bouts, but you also started the odd boxing bout, and have been both a fighter and a referee."

"I used to box when I was at the United States Naval Academy at Annapolis," George explained.

"He was the champion," Stanley added. "And he never lost a bout in Tombstone, despite being up against some of these miners who are all solid muscle."

George stroked his mustache. "Science, Stanley. Boxing is an art and a science. Don't lose your temper, but be scientific in the way you fight, those are my personal rules."

Carrie stared up at George with wide-eyed amazement. "I can't believe that our doctor used to be a boxer."

Stanley stood up and Carrie did likewise. "Well, dear, I wouldn't be surprised if Doctor Goodfellow didn't have a go at arm-wrestling again this evening."

Carrie giggled anew.

The Medley of Shakespeare Scenes performed by The Strolling Players Theater Troup was less than spectacular, George thought. He had met Stanley and Carlton in the foyer and they had a drink at the bar before taking their seats. While George enjoyed a little Shakespeare when it was done well, he could barely tolerate it when it was acted badly.

And the Strolling Players Theater Troup performed so poorly that the audience started to boo and slow handclap. It was not the boisterous and demonstrative booing that performers at the Bird Cage Theater had to put up with, when eggs, fruit or even bottles could be tossed at them, yet it was enough to make the players curtail their performance and cancel the following night's performance.

But it allowed George, Stanley and Carlton to head for the Oriental Saloon earlier than they had intended.

Over a beer at the bar George asked about Esme.

"She's still poorly, George. I'm getting a bit worried about her actually. I wanted her to see Doctor Matthews while you were away, but she straight refused. I wasn't going to come this evening either, but she insisted that I did."

"I'll call on her tomorrow," George said, reassuringly. "Which brings me to another matter. Edith would like to attend school here until she goes back East. I think it would distract her from losing her mother."

"Plus, my Carrie would welcome her and make sure she settles in," said Stanley.

"I can't see any reason why not. Just bring her along in the morning."

"Excellent! Your good health, gentlemen."

They clinked glasses and drained them. George signaled to the barkeeper for refills.

While the barkeeper tended to the order one of the other bartenders, known to everyone as Abe, banged a bottle on the counter to gain everyone's attention in the crowded saloon.

"Roll up, gents! Roll up. Time for the arm wrestling competition. Anyone can enter for a dollar. We'll put names in a hat, each pair of competitors will have the best of three bouts and it will be a knockout competition." He tossed a piece of chalk in the air and tapped a blackboard on the wall. "I'll do the draw here so it is all aboveboard and fair."

He spotted George and raised his voice. "And we have Doctor Goodfellow himself here this evening, men. As you know, he was our undefeated champion for a whole year a few years ago. Will you look after any injuries, sir?"

"As long as I get a fee," George returned. "And anyone who doesn't pay a fee will get their other arm twisted by me!"

His joke occasioned general banter and hilarity, much to George's further enjoyment.

The barkeeper laughed. "Can we tempt you to enter the competition yourself, sir?"

George shook his head. "I'll stick to watching, doctoring and drinking this evening, thanks Abe."

"And what about you sir, Mister Levine?" Abe called out. "You are a strong looking fellow and you look as if you could give the good doctor a run for his money?"

Carlton shook his head with a modest laugh. "It's a bit too physical for my taste. I'm the bookish type and I prefer other games."

"Plenty of other games here, sir," Abe shouted back. "Right ladies?"

Several of the saloon girls gave coquettish gestures and a couple made lewd remarks, which sent a wave of raucous laughter around the saloon.

"Or what about you, Mister Bagg?" Abe went on, enjoying the response he was obtaining from the saloon clientele. "Would you care to part with a dollar and try your arm at wrestling?"

At five foot tall Stanley was used to being the butt of saloon humor. He didn't let it bother him, since he knew that he could hold his own in any verbal battle. "No, I'll just watch and make notes. And report on the standard of entertainment in a column tomorrow."

Abe took the message and switched attention back to the blackboard and the top hat that he had placed on the bar in readiness to receive names of the arm wrestlers.

The competition started in earnest at several tables, each of which accumulated a crowd as friends and well-wishers jostled each other to get a clear view and to urge on their chosen champion. As was the way of such saloon antics, apart from the purse that the arm-wrestlers were vying for there were several other books going on. There were some seriously strong miners and cowboys chancing their arms and accordingly there was much money riding on each bout.

George, Stanley and Carlton looked on from the bar.

"Are you tempted, George?" Stanley asked, looking up at his friend.

"Not a bit."

"Well, what did you think about Abe's remark," Carlton asked, "do you think I'd give you a run for your money?"

"Are you challenging me, Carlton?" George responded in surprise.

"Just joshing. I suppose I'm wondering how I would fare myself against some of these man-mountains."

"You could always drop your dollar in the hat," George said. "Abe will accept another entrant at this stage."

Stanley shook his head. "Typical! The trial of

strength impulse is a hanger on from the days of the cavemen. But it isn't brawn that made mankind so successful, it was his brain."

George laughed. "Spoken like a true newspaperman and man of letters."

"But it is true, George. The pen is mightier than the sword. That means that the man who thinks fastest wins. We could always put it to the test."

Carlton sipped his beer. "What are you proposing, Stanley?"

"Chess! Let's the three of us have a competition right here. You both play, don't you?"

"You know we do, Stanley, although I haven't played in a couple of years," George said, filling his pipe. "But the last I heard the Oriental Saloon only runs to gambling games. There may be a checkers board, but I doubt if there will be a chess set."

"In that case, give me a few minutes and I'll go and get mine," Stanley said, replacing his beer on the counter and heading off through the crowds.

"Well, Carlton, I guess we'll have to humor Stanley. Watch out though, he may be a small fellow, but like a lot of little chaps he can be as competitive as hell."

"I know, George. He certainly doesn't mince his words in his columns in either the *Prospector* or the *Epitaph*. He wields his pen like it was a saber."

"Do you play much chess?"

"Oh, you know me, George. I like all board games."

George snapped his fingers. "Of course, you were teaching the children about tactics, weren't you?"

"I was, but I hasten to add that I'm nowhere near as good a chess player as Esme. She can plot a game four or even five moves ahead."

"Remind me never to play her then," said George, striking a light to his pipe. "Let's head over to that table in the corner. It won't be any quieter, but at least we will be less likely to get jostled."

Indeed, the noise from around the saloon was getting louder and louder as the competitors fought, gradually whittling the numbers down.

Stanley returned and spotted them in the corner. He came over and lay the chessboard on the table.

"Right gentlemen," he said, as he set out the pieces. "I suggest we have a round robin competition. Each of us plays the other two."

"And we each put in what, five dollars?" George suggested.

"A confident man," joked Carlton. "How about making it ten?"

"Have some confidence in your ability, gentlemen, let's make it fifty," said Stanley, as he left to collect his drink from the bar.

George winked at Carlton. "See what I mean?"

When he returned, Stanley pushed his wire-framed spectacles back on his nose and lit a fresh cigar.

He coughed then raised his hand. "Not a word, George Goodfellow! I know cigars don't help my chest, but they help me concentrate. And this is a concentrating game."

"What happens if we each win a game and all end up with one win?" Carlton asked.

"Then we all play each other again, until we have an outright winner," Stanley replied.

"And what if one of us wins twice and one wins once?" George queried.

"Then the two times winner takes one hundred dollars and the one time winner takes fifty. The two time loser gets nothing."

And so, the principle established, it began.

It did not take long before some of the arm-wrestling spectators drifted away from the tables and started to congregate around the chess players. Soon folks were cheering and urging George and Stanley on. Clearly, most folks had little idea what the game involved for they thought that gusto and encouragement would be bound to help.

"Quieten down folks!" George snapped. "This isn't like arm-wrestling you know. A player needs to think, and to think he needs some peace and quiet. Now shush!"

He moved his bishop across the board, noticing

too late that he had opened up a hole in his defense. Stanley had anticipated it, however, and moved in to take the game five moves later.

And so Stanley notched up his game against George and promptly reset the pieces to take on Carlton.

This match was quicker than the one with George. Indeed, George noted the different styles of play by his opponents. Stanley played classically, aiming to control the middle of the board. Carlton on the other hand played the so-called Romantic way. He was attacking, bold and determined always to win or lose with panache.

Again, Stanley was the victor, which left George and Carlton to play for the second prize.

George noted that Carlton was using the Sicilian Defense, which suited his style of play. Accordingly, he tried to play like Stanley and establish mastery over the center board.

But Carlton was unpredictable. He sacrificed a bishop and then a knight, giving George a smug glow.

Too smug, because he missed the check and before he knew it, it was checkmate.

Cheers went up from the crowd, who inexplicably had switched allegiance from the brawny arm-wrestling to watch the brain-powered chess tournament. Much to his discomfiture, Stanley was hoisted aloft and carried upon many hefty shoulders to the bar, where he was deposited on top, as if it was a stage.

"Well, I guess the beer is on me," he called out. "Just one each, though!"

There was a rapid move of people to the bar.

Carlton stuffed his fifty dollars back in his wallet. "Hard luck, George. Stanley got the better of us tonight."

"There was no luck involved, Carlton. The little fellow sand-bagged us, I think. And you outplayed me, too. I reckon I'll call it a night. I'll drop Edith at the school tomorrow, then I'll call in to see Esme. Good night."

George shouldered his way through the crowd, noticing that the finalists of the arm-wrestling were still straining against one another, watched by a few stragglers. But he was not in a good mood. Although he did not begrudge Stanley his victory, he did resent the way that the saloon crowd were fawning over him. It was something that he was used to and he hated to admit it to himself, but he was not a good loser.

# Chapter 9
## LUCREZIA

Edith was in a high state of excitement the next morning when George walked her to school.

"This is going to be the best of days, Daddy," she said as she held onto his hand.

"I am sure it will be, Princess. You will probably know all of the other pupils, or at least know them by sight. It may be strange having other children of different ages in the same class, but Tombstone is still a young town and the school hasn't had time to develop like the one you are used to."

"It's going to be fun, Daddy. And as you often say, it is good to experience different things."

They walked turned the corner and saw a group of children waiting outside the schoolhouse at Fourth and Toughnut Streets. Right next door was the Tombstone Library, which had been built in 1885 and run by George's friend George Whitewell Parsons. Parsons had been injured in a fire in the Abbot House, when he got caught on the balcony. A wood beam fell and struck him in the face, smashing his nose and breaking his jaw. George operated on him several times, improvising operations as he went on and effectively rebuilt his nose. The whole town had been saddened when he left a couple of years later, for he had established the Tombstone Library and put it on a firm footing.

Carrie spotted them coming along and waved. Then she pulled a couple of girls that she had been chatting with and ran to meet them.

"Edith, this is great. You'll like it here. This is Isabel and this is Dorothy."

George grinned as the trio surrounded Edith and instantly they were all chattering away.

The school door opened and Carlton came out, holding a large handbell in one hand. Behind him was Fiona Parker.

"Ah, George, you have brought Edith," Carlton said. "Excuse me one moment while I ring the bell."

As he rang it, the children, of whom there were about twenty-five of various ages up to teenagers, went quiet and then filed in past him in an orderly, well practiced manner.

"Welcome Edith," he said as Edith, Carrie, Isabel and Dorothy walked in. "Have a seat beside Carrie and I'll introduce you to the class when I come in. Missus Parker is going to be teaching with us this morning."

As Carlton spoke George noted that he had slightly bloodshot eyes. It was likely that he had caught conjunctivitis from the librarian.

"Good morning, Missus Parker," George said, tipping his hat to her.

"Good morning, Doctor Goodfellow," she replied with a smile before turning and following the children inside.

"We'll look after her, don't worry, George."

"You are looking a bit worried yourself, Carlton."

Carlton nodded. "I think Esme's illness is getting to me, George. She isn't getting any better, is she?"

"I'll make her my first call after my morning surgery."

"Do you know what's wrong? It seems more than a stomach upset."

George maintained his poker face. Esme Levine had not wanted him to tell Carlton anything and he had to respect that. "Medical things are not always straightforward, Carlton. I'll see what I can do today."

The schoolteacher bit his lip and nodded. George patted his arm reassuringly and then headed off along Toughnut Street. He didn't mention Carlton's conjunctivitis.

His surgery that morning was not busy so he was able to visit Esme Levine earlier than he thought he would.

He found her in bed, leaning back against a bank of pillows. There was a smell of vomit and he noted the bowl on the floor.

"Carlton tells me that he wanted to get Doctor

Matthews to see you while I was away, Esme."

"I only wanted to see you, Doctor Goodfellow. I only trust you."

"So how are you feeling? Any better."

She shook her head. "I'm still sick every day and I can't eat. My throat burns and these abdominal pains keep coming." She sighed and touched her head. "And I think I am losing my hair. More and more seems to be just falling out."

"You are losing weight as well, I think. Can I examine you?"

As he did he found her abdomen to be tender and the abdominal mass was either slightly larger, or the same but easier to feel, because of the weight loss.

"Esme, I think that surgery is the only answer here. You must let me operate."

"No!" she said firmly.

"Then you should at least come into hospital."

She shook her head. "No hospital."

"Then I need to have a frank talk with Carlton. He needs to know. I saw him at school this morning and he asked me what was wrong with you."

She bit her lip and shook her head again. "No, I don't want him to know."

"But why? He is understandably very concerned about you. And if this lump in your abdomen is malignant, then he has a right to know what can happen."

"You mean, he needs to know that I am going to die?"

"Yes. He needs to know that it is a possibility."

She turned her face away and let out a sob. "The thing is . . . it may be for the best. I . . . I don't think he would care."

"That's not true. He's worried sick. In fact, I believe he may be getting ill himself." George thought that the conjunctivitis could be a sign that his health was starting to fail. He was all too well aware that people often picked up infections when they were run down with worry.

"I am sorry," she said. "Perhaps you could give me some more of that medicine. It seems to help a little."

"Are you still having your beef tea?"

She nodded. "Carlton makes it for me. I can manage that and some soup now and then. Oh, and those delicious cinnamon and arrowroot biscuits that he brings me from Fiona Parker."

"Well, both cinnamon and arrowroot are good for upset stomachs. They are probably helping."

He recalled that her cat Tabitha enjoyed them.

"Where is your cat? He's usually your companion, isn't he?"

Tears welled up in her eyes. "He . . . he was. But he's gone and Carlton can't find him anywhere."

"That's cats for you. I've had several cats and all of them would take off for days on end.

I'm sure she'll be back in her own good time."

Before leaving his surgery George had made up more bottles of Bismuthi Subcarbonas and Laudanum et Asafoetidae. He took them out of his black bag and placed them on the bedside table.

"Just take these exactly as before. I'll call back tomorrow. But please reconsider about the operation and about letting me talk to Carlton."

He heard her start to cry as he let himself out of the house.

That evening Edith was full of news about her first day at the Tombstone School.

"Missus Parker is just so sweet. She seems to know lots and lots. She taught the girls about Household Management, while Mister Levine was teaching the boys mathematics."

George sipped his coffee. "That reminds me, Stella. I saw Missus Parker yesterday and she was telling me about this book that she thinks every woman ought to know about. It was called *Mrs. Beeton's Book of Household Management*. It is a British book, but she has copies in the library and if you are interested she will put one aside for you."

"She showed us the book today," Edith said. "It's a huge thick book, like one of your medical books, Daddy."

"I have heard of it," said Stella. "It is full of

thousands of recipes and advice about running a house, and even about how to treat people."

George laughed. "Yes, so I gather. She told me that after I gave her an ointment."

"She is going to teach us about the chemistry of soups," Edith announced.

"Chemistry of soup?" Stella repeated. "Making soup is cooking not chemistry."

"Nothing wrong with a scientific approach to cooking, Stella," George said with a smile.

"Oh you and your science. I might have guessed you would stick up for that. Mind you, I wouldn't mind having a look at this book."

"Then I shall ask her tomorrow when I take Edith to school."

Talking about science stimulated George to go and do some work on his research into making a bulletproof vest. Once settled in his study he laid his notes and jottings out on the desk and then filled and lit his pipe.

And as he sat thinking about bullets his mind turned to Doctor John Handy. Immediately he felt a twinge of guilt again and started to mentally berate himself for failing to save his friend.

"You could have done with a few layers of silk, John," he mused. He shook his head. "Such a waste of talent."

And then he recalled the argument that he had with Stella about Dr. Handy and Gila Monsters. Stella had been convinced that John had said they were poisonous. He remembered him recounting how Walter Vail, the owner of the Empire Ranch was riding near Pantano and clubbed a Gila Monster. Thinking that it was dead he tied it to his saddle to take to a friend. Then the Gila woke up and he tried to prod it away, only for it to bite and latch onto his finger. He tried to free himself, but it wouldn't let go. He got back to his ranch house and one of his men prized its jaws apart with a knife.

Apparently he felt really ill and so he was taken straight to Tucson, where they sought out Dr. John Handy, who treated him in the usual manner, by incising the wound to let the flow of blood carry out the poison and then cauterized it. Vail was ill for days, John said, with swollen and bleeding glands in his neck, but he survived.

It irked George that he couldn't remember whether John had actually said that he thought Gilas were poisonous or not. And it irked him that so many folk thought that they were dangerous and shot them on sight.

He had been incensed by a paper in the *Scientific American* journal of the year before saying that the Gila Monster's breath was fetid and that it was this foul smelling gas that overcame insects and small animals so that it could catch them. He had thought this to be just another of the myths about the creatures, hence he started collecting and studying them.

"Damn it! I'd better go and check on my little collection of them."

None of them were visible in their enclosures, so he opened up Lucrezia's gate and stepped in.

"Where are you, Lucrezia?" he said, clicking his tongue as if to tempt the largest of the Gilas out of her cave. Then he mentally castigated himself.

"What the hell am I doing? It's a reptile not a dog." And he bent down and peered inside.

Lucrezia was there. She was lying motionless in the shadows of her little cave.

"Darn. You're not dead are you? Edith would be heartbroken."

He reached in and prodded her side.

He was not prepared for the speed of her attack. Before he knew it she had bitten him on the forefinger and would not let go.

"Gah! Let go, you brute," he said as he pulled his arm out with the Gila firmly attached to his finger.

He struck it on the head with his other hand and then tried to open its jaws. But she still would not let go.

"I'm a surgeon and I need my fingers," he said between gritted teeth. He reached behind his back for his Italian poniard dagger. "And so . . ."

He was about to stab her when she suddenly let go and scuttled back into her cave.

George stared at the throbbing finger with

the teeth marks that were already oozing blood. He was about to suck the finger, then stopped himself.

"I don't believe they are as poisonous as everyone says," he said to himself. "I'll treat this scientifically, first with a good wash with water and carbolic, then with a magnesium sulfate poultice to draw any venom out, and then I'll take painkiller."

He wrapped a handkerchief around it as a first measure then let himself out of the enclosure and strode back to the house.

"Daddy, have you been checking on Lucrezia and Socrates and the others?" Edith asked.

"Yes, they are all fine, Princess," he said, tousling her hair with his left hand as he passed her.

"Are you all right, Doctor Goodfellow, sir?" Stella asked, having noticed that his right hand was stuffed firmly in his pocket.

"Perfectly fine, thank you, Stella," he said, collecting his medical bag from the hall stand as he went back to his study.

Once on his own he dressed the finger then poured himself a large whiskey before returning to his desk.

"Whiskey is the best painkiller for me. Now let's just see what happens. I reckon I'll know soon enough if Lucrezia deserves her name as a poisoner."

And he sat and sipped his whiskey, ready to begin recording any symptoms.

Despite the whiskey the whole of his hand was starting to hurt and he was beginning to feel light-headed.

# Chapter 10
## YELLOW SLUDGE

George woke up with a slight headache after a fitful night in bed. He was aware that he had been dreaming vividly, but as often happened with him the content of the dreams disappeared like smoke upon waking.

The headache he attributed to the whiskey he had drunk in his study while he waited to see whether he was going to experience any effects from Gila venom.

He threw back his blanket and swung his legs out of bed. He looked at his bandaged finger. The whole hand was painful, but there was no sign of inflammation tracking up his arm.

"That's good. There's no sign of lymphangitis so there won't be any gland swelling." He stood up and shook his head.

"And other than this little headache I have no light-headedness. All looking good."

He pulled on a dressing gown and went through to his study where he sat and made notes about how he felt. Later on he would collate it with his other researches about the Gila Monsters.

There was a tap on his door and Edith put her head around it. She was already dressed and ready for school. But he noted the worried look on her face.

"Good morning, Daddy. Could you come and look at Lucrezia? She's lying half in and half outside her cave. She doesn't look well. I'm worried that she may have eaten something that has upset her."

George could barely suppress a grin. Maybe Doctor George Goodfellow was poisonous to Gilas.

"I'll come and look at her now, Princess."

But as he stood up he had a strange sense of foreboding. It was as if some dream image of the night before, something that had been troubling him was demanding his attention.

Carlton was outside the school talking to Stanley Bagg when George arrived with Edith.

Carrie and her friends Dorothy and Isabel immediately greeted Edith and included her in their chatter.

George noted that Carton's conjunctivitis was looking worse.

"Are you taking anything for that eye infection?" he asked.

"That's just what I asked him," said Stanley.

"No, it will go, I am sure," Carlton replied airily. "These things don't last long with me." He nodded at George's bandaged finger. "But what have you done, George?"

"Oh nothing. Just trapped my finger in a door, he lied evasively, for he had no desire for Edith to know that he had provoked Lucrezia into biting him. It had been all that he could do to reassure her that the Gila wasn't ill.

"Will you . . . will you be going to see Esme?" Carlton asked.

"Right after my surgery."

"Could, er . . . could you go before it? I wanted to stay with her this morning, but she insisted that I go to work."

"Of course, Carlton. I have my bag here, so I'll go straight there."

"I'll walk with you, George," said Stanley. "I have to drop in to see the Reverend Franklin at St Paul's Episcopal Church. I'm doing a piece for the *Epitaph* about strange noises and lights that have been heard and seen in the church after dark."

"Good luck on that, then," Carlton said with a sneer. "We live across the street from it and I suspect that any noises and lights the Reverend Franklin has experienced are the result of imbibing too much rye whiskey."

And raising his handbell he rang it to bring the children into school.

George found Esme in bed as usual. She looked miserable and she had clearly been crying. She had dark rings around her sunken eyes.

"I . . . I feel so unwell, Doctor," she moaned.

"Still being sick?"

"And . . . and I have the runs."

"Anything else?"

"I am breathless when I get up."

George opened his bag and pulled out his stethoscope. "Let me listen to your heart and chest, Esme."

It took him a few minutes to complete his examination. He coiled his stethoscope up and replaced it in the bag.

"You have some swelling of your ankles, Esme, and you are starting to get fluid in your lungs. This is dropsy that you are getting now. That means that your heart is starting to find it hard to pump blood around your body."

He looked at her tongue.

"Have you had soup?"

"No, Doctor, I couldn't face it last night."

"Any beef tea?"

"Yes, Carlton makes me have it. And my cinnamon and arrowroot biscuits are the only solid food that I can manage."

"Does Carlton put garlic in your beef tea?" George asked with narrowed eyes.

"No, he just makes it as plain as possible."

Once again, George experienced a strange sense of foreboding.

He picked up her vomit bowl and stared at the contents. Then he sniffed it.

"Tell me truthfully, Esme, how long have you been feeling melancholic?"

She looked down at her hands, which George noted were trembling. "For . . . for a long time."

"Since when, Esme?"

"For about a year, it's been getting worse. Ever since it became obvious that Carlton no longer loved me and that he wanted someone else."

"Who is that, Esme?"

"I . . . I think you probably know the answer, Doctor."

"Missus Parker?"

As he said it, it all seemed to make sense. Carlton and Fiona Parker, both teaching at the school, and when she wasn't helping she was just next door in the Tombstone Library. And she had recently consulted him with conjunctivitis, only for Carlton to have developed it himself over the last couple of days. It was likely that they had been close in the last days or two. Very close, like when kissing, or more.

That sense of foreboding just got ten times worse.

"Yes, Fiona Parker. I think he . . . he loves her. She is all he would talk about for weeks, then he stopped talking about her. That's when I started to get suspicious that he might be in love with her. That he might be . . . having a liaison with her."

"I can't see that, Esme. Carlton is always so

concerned about you. He seems to really care for you."

She raised a hand to her mouth and bit the back of her knuckle. "I . . . I think that is what he would like everyone to believe."

"And this recent illness, how long have you been ill?"

"Vomiting and abdominal pains, really bad for a few weeks, but I've been unwell for about a couple of months, just getting worse. Is it a cancer, Doctor? Is this breathlessness and dropsy a result of that?"

George had felt constricted in what Esme was prepared to let him say to Carlton, now he felt he had to hold back about what was in his mind.

"I am afraid that it is possible, Esme. But I need to do some tests. I have an idea. I want to take that vomit bowl of yours."

"Of course. Whatever you need. Just tell me, Doctor Goodfellow, will it be painful . . . when . . . when it . . ."

George laid a hand on her shoulder. "It is too soon to talk about that, Esme."

He found a flannel and draped it over the bowl, then picked up his bag ready to go.

"It isn't that I'm afraid of death, Doctor," Esme said, leaning back against her pillows. "In fact, I think I . . . I will welcome it."

George patted her hand. "You must try not to

think like that. Look, I will do some tests after my surgery this morning and then I will come back to see you as soon as I can. And then I am going to talk to your husband."

Stanley was just coming out of St Paul's Episcopal Church as George left the Levine house.

"Ah Stanley, just the man. Can you come over to my surgery about eleven o'clock? I'd like you to witness something."

"Of course. You look serious, George. Anything wrong?"

"Maybe something seriously wrong."

"Is there a story in it for me?"

George clicked his tongue. "There may be, but then again, there might be a story that you won't care to publish."

The surgery was busier than George would have liked, but that was often his experience the longer he practiced medicine. When you were under pressure then more patients with more complex needs turned up to heap more pressure on you. In the course of the morning he had to lance three boils, remove a splinter of metal from the blacksmith's eye, listen to the troubles and woes of half a dozen folk who were afflicted with melancholia or nervous anxiety, and make up and dispense several tonics, elixirs and fever powders.

Stanley was sitting in the waiting room when he showed his last patient out.

"Please come through to the dispensing room, Stanley," he said as he locked the waiting room door.

"You are not going to show me anything disgusting are you, George? I can get a mite squeamish you know."

George pointed to one of the two chairs by his dispensing bench. Stanley sat down and looked at the array of bottles, flasks and chemistry paraphernalia.

From a cupboard George took out a strange looking piece of glass apparatus, consisting of three glass globes that seemed to be stacked on top of each other, but which were interconnected by a glass tube that ran down inside from the top to the bottom globe. A rubber tube with a stopcock halfway along it was connected to a spout protruding from the middle globe.

"This is a Kipp generator for producing gases," George explained, as he poured a powder into a special cylinder inside the middle globe. "This chemical is iron sulfide."

"This dispensary of yours is probably as well equipped as the assayer's laboratory," Stanley remarked, pointing at the spring balance George used for weighing drugs and remedy ingredients.

"It is indeed," George replied nonchalantly. "I do all my own assays, Stanley, just as my father used to do. He taught me more chemistry than I was ever shown in medical school."

He assembled a few bottles of liquid in readiness.

"So is this another of your experiments you want me to see, George?"

"It is not an experiment, it is a test I'm going to do, Stanley. I just feel that I need a witness to confirm whatever result I get. But before I begin, I want you to smell something."

He reached under the bench and took out the bowl of vomit. "What does this smell like to you, Stanley?" he asked as he whipped away the flannel.

The newspaperman leaned forward with closed eyes and sniffed gingerly.

"Garlic, I think. Yes, definitely, garlic."

"That's what I thought, too. This is Esme Levine's vomit bowl."

"So what does that tell you, George? That she has been eating garlic?"

"She is barely eating, Stanley. And she says that she hasn't had any food with garlic in it. Now let's do that test." He picked up one of the bottles and poured liquid into the topmost globe.

"Have you heard of a man called Doctor Samuel Hahnemann?"

Stanley had a prodigious memory for obscure information. "Yes, he was the doctor who founded that discipline of medicine called homeopathy, wasn't he? As far as I know it is all about giving very dilute amounts of things to stimulate healing in the patient."

"Very good, Stanley. That is exactly right. I am not sure that I agree with the principles, myself. It doesn't seem to make sense that the more dilute something is, the more effective it gets, but that is what homeopathic doctors believe. But that isn't why I mention him. It is because the man was a great chemist and he introduced one of the most effective tests for a specific metal. Let's see if it works."

He kept pouring fluid into the top globe until he was satisfied there was enough.

"This liquid is sulfuric acid," he explained. "Now watch what happens when I release the stopcock here. When I do that the air inside the middle chamber is expelled and the liquid in the top will flow right down to the bottom container."

Stanley watched with fascination as the liquid did just that and rose up in the base and then up into the middle globe, where it started to fizz when it met the iron sulfide powder. Then suddenly he sat back. "Good heavens, George, what is that? It smells like bad eggs."

"Exactly right, Stanley. In the flask the sulfuric acid and the iron sulphide react to produce iron sulfate and a gas called hydrogen sulfide. That is the bad egg smell."

He closed the stopcock on the rubber tube and Stanley saw that the level of liquid in the middle chamber started to fall and that liquid was forced back up into the top globe.

"As more of the gas is produced it pushes the acid back into the top reservoir," George explained. "We don't need too much of it."

He then filled a flat-bottomed conical flask with some of the vomitus from the bowl.

"This is the fiddly bit, Stanley. Especially with my finger all bandaged up. I now add some dilute hydrochloric acid to the stomach contents here. Then we pass some of the hydrogen sulfide gas through it."

He put the end of the rubber tube into the flask. "If what I suspect is true, Stanley, you will see a yellow precipitate start to form. That is, you'll see some yellow sludge."

He opened the stopcock and the foul smelling gas started to bubble through the vomit liquid. Almost immediately a yellow precipitate started to form."

Stanley started to smile. "Congratulations, George. You were right. So what—?"

But George was not smiling. He was scowling.

"Damn it! That was what I didn't want to find," he said as he turned the stopcock off. "That yellow sludge is arsenic sulfide. It proves my worst fear. Our friend Carlton Levine has been poisoning his wife with arsenic."

# Chapter 11
## THE MISSING CAT

Stanley stared at George in disbelief. "You are kidding me?"

"It is hardly a joking matter, Stanley." He held up his hand with the bandaged finger. "I've been blinkered for so long, I am afraid. See my finger. I let Lucrezia, one of my Gila Monsters, bite me. I was convinced a Gila bite can't kill you and that it would not be any more poisonous than any other creature's bite. Well, I was right, it hasn't done any more than give me a painful and slightly puffed up hand, but I have to admit it did have some poison in it. The point is that it is not enough to be fatal."

"I don't see what that has to do with Carlton and him poisoning his wife?"

"It has been staring me in the face for days, Stanley. I should have recognized the symptoms, but because she has a medical condition, I chose not to think the worst, that my friend was slowly poisoning her with arsenic in her beef tea."

"There's no doubt?"

"I am afraid not."

"Then we need to inform Marshal Steadman?"

George shook his head. "Jerry Steadman is in

bed with a broken leg. I splinted it last week. No, let's go and tell Sheriff Kelton. I think this will be a matter for the Cochise County Sheriff to investigate. He and the town marshal work together anyway, so he can arrest Carlton. Then I need to get back to see Esme."

Sheriff C.B. Kelton was an upright, no-nonsense lawman of the old school. He had taken on the job after Camillus Fly, the town's photographer and another of George's friends had served for two years.

George and Stanley had both gone straight to his office in the Cochise County Courthouse on Toughnut Street. It was a grand fire red brick two-storied structure that had been built in 1882 in the form of a cross and which housed the Cochise County Courtroom, the sheriff's office, the recorder's office and the jailhouse.

Sheriff Kelton twirled an end of his long white mustache as he listened in disbelief to the town doctor and the newspaper editor's tale.

"Hell if that isn't the most ornery thing I've heard in a long time. And this Hahnemann test is surefire, Doc?"

"It is accurate, but there is a more sophisticated one called the Marsh test. I've never used that, whereas I knew how to do this one. But there is plenty more of the vomit if you want to get it analyzed by someone else."

"Not yet, but I may do. The first thing I need to do is go see Missus Levine. While I do that I'll get my deputy, Bill Meade to go and arrest Levine and bring him to the house."

And so the sheriff, George and Stanley rode back to the Levine house in the sheriff's buggy.

Esme was understandably surprised and somewhat overawed, when the three men came into her bedroom.

"I have brought the sheriff, Esme. I have bad news for you. I did the test I said I was going to do on your vomit bowl and I found it contained arsenic."

"Arsenic?" she repeated, aghast. "But . . . but that's not possible. It . . . it is poisonous, isn't it?"

"It is, Esme. That is why I brought Mister Bagg, who witnessed me doing the test, and the sheriff."

Sheriff Kelton stepped forward. If he felt awkward he did not show it. He laid his hat on a chair and got straight to the matter. "Missus Levine, it is my belief that your husband has been poisoning your beef tea."

Esme gasped and covered her face. Then she fainted.

Carlton Levine stood at the end of Esme's bed, his face ashen white and his lips trembling. His wrists were cuffed and Deputy Bill Meade stood a pace behind him. George had revived Esme with a dose of smelling salts and she stared at her husband with a mixture of shock and horror.

"It . . . it all makes sense now," she almost whispered. "How . . . how could you, Carlton?"

"Esme, I swear, I didn't."

Sheriff Kelton nodded at George. "Doc Goodfellow here says there is plenty of arsenic in that vomit bowl. How do you account for that, Levine?"

Carlton Levine was flustered. "I . . . I have not—"

"Did you hate me so much, Carlton?" Esme asked.

"I don't hate you at all, Esme."

She stared at him for a moment then turned her head and sobbed. "I loved you and would have done anything for you, yet you did this."

"Esme, please. There must be some logical explanation for this."

"Yes, Carlton, there must," she replied, turning and looking straight at him. "If you haven't been poisoning me, then who has?"

Sheriff Kelton jabbed a finger towards Carlton. "Well, Levine, did you do this or not? Have you been poisoning your wife?"

The schoolteacher stared helplessly at his wife for a moment, then looked pleadingly at George and Stanley, his friends.

"And you . . . you killed Tabitha, my cat!" she cried.

Carlton Levine stared at her with eyes open wide in the alarm of discovery. He gave a loud sigh and his shoulders slumped.

"I . . . I admit it," he said, bowing his head and bursting into tears. "I did it. I tried to kill my wife."

Sheriff Kelton suppressed a curse. "You poor excuse for a man. Take him to the jailhouse, Bill. As quick as you can."

George waited while everyone else had gone. "Esme, I am so sorry. I never thought that Carlton would be capable of anything like that."

She had dissolved into tears. "Oh Doctor Goodfellow, if you only knew what he was capable of! If you only knew."

"Esme, now that I know what has been wrong with you, I can tell you that you will get better. It is just going to take time. I have some other patients to see, but I will call back later."

The whole of Tombstone was shocked at the news that spread as fast as wildfire. In every shop, office, saloon and home, it was the sole topic of conversation for the next two days.

The hearing was held by Judge James Robinson, a martinet of the law with a black spade beard and ice cold eyes that peered from behind thick spectacles. The courtroom was packed to capacity.

Everyone in town had sympathy for Esme

Levine, who was not present, being deemed too ill still to attend.

Carlton Levine had refused legal representation and sat with his head bowed as the charges were read out.

"To the charges against you, how do you plead?" Judge Robinson asked. "Guilty or not guilty?"

"Guilty!" Carlton replied calmly. "I am guilty."

"Then there is nothing for it. The court accepts your admission and I will retire for half an hour to consider everything and then I shall pass sentence."

He rapped his gavel and everyone stood while he left the court.

As the crowd filed out with many an angry muttering, having been deprived of the spectacle of a proper trial, George caught Stanley's arm.

"Are you going to run an article on this?" he asked.

"Of course. The people have a right to know everything. And to tell you the truth, George, I am disgusted. I feel betrayed by him. Goodness only knows what his poor wife feels."

"I feel bad that I just didn't see it and that she suffered so much because of it."

"George, any man that could do something like that deserves whatever is coming to him. I'm going to write that article as soon as we know what the judge decides. Personally, I think hanging might be too good for him."

George winced, for he was not prepared for Stanley's vindictive outburst. He still found it hard to convince himself that the Carlton Levine he had been friends with the past few years could have been slowly poisoning his wife.

Half an hour later the court reconvened and Judge Robinson summed up and passed sentence.

"You will be taken to the Yuma Territorial Prison, where I sentence you to thirty years hard labor. Sheriff Kelton will arrange to have you taken there by prison wagon tomorrow."

Carlton Levine sat through it and merely nodded his head. He looked at no one when he was led away.

George joined the throng as everyone filed out again. This time the hostility and anger was almost palpable. Many people were muttering that Carlton Levine ought to be hanged.

George spent the afternoon in his surgery, listening to the opinions of his patients as he diagnosed and treated them.

Fiona Parker was among them.

"Ah, your eyes seem better now, Missus Parker."

"They are, Doctor, thank you. I just . . . I just wanted to ask how Missus Levine is?"

"Why don't you call and see her yourself?"

"I don't think she would welcome me. You see,

I—was, that is, I mean I am very close to Carlton. I don't know what we will do without him. The school is closed, of course."

"I understand. Well, she is still very ill, but I am hopeful that she will start to pick up now that she is no longer taking poison into her system. Stella, my housekeeper calls in to see her every afternoon to make sure she tries to have some food. She still refuses to come into hospital."

"I hope she gets better soon. Could you pass on my best wishes when you see her next?"

"Of course I will."

She looked as if she wanted to say more, but with a demure nod of her head, she left.

The mood in town seemed to be getting more and more heated as the saloons did a roaring trade and their clientele drank themselves into an indignant furor. That evening about eight o'clock Stanley called on George's surgery after he finished work and they had gone for a drink in the Oriental Saloon.

"I can't say that I like the talk that is going around," George said.

"No, nor do I," Stanley agreed. "I may have been over-verbal myself this morning, but I calmed down as I wrote my article. Now I simply can't believe that the three of us were last in here playing chess."

At the thought of their chess competition

George immediately had a strange feeling of foreboding, not dissimilar to the ones he had before, when Edith had been worried about Lucrezia and when he started to suspect that Esme Levine's illness might have been due to poison.

He lit his pipe and blew a stream of blue smoke upwards to merge into the tobacco smoke haze that hung over the saloon.

"Come over to the table we were playing chess at, Stanley. I want to knock a few ideas around in the air."

They took their drinks to the corner table.

"First off, I'm worried about the way folks are talking. I can remember when folks got riled up back in 1883 when John Heath was lynched on Toughnut Street. That happened when folks got liquored up like this. It would just need a rabble-rouser to start it off, especially when Carlton's being taken to Yuma tomorrow."

"Sheriff Kelton would never let that happen."

"No, but when you talked about chess that set me off thinking, Stanley. What if Carlton is innocent?"

"What are you talking about, George. You did that Hahnemann test. You proved that there was arsenic in Esme Levine's system."

"Yes, but I assumed it was from the beef tea that Carlton was making her."

"What else could it have been?"

"I think I know," George said, snapping

his fingers. "I should have realized when she mentioned the cat. She said that he had killed her cat."

"I don't understand, George."

"No, of course you don't. How could you? The thing is that Esme Levine had a cat called Tabitha that used to lie on her bed. A few days ago it went missing."

"So what is all this to do with chess?"

"Carlton's chess style, Stanley. He uses the Italian style. All flamboyance. He sacrifices pieces to distract you into missing a move. That's what he has done here. He has sacrificed himself."

"For who?"

"For Fiona Parker."

"Why? Tell me what you are thinking."

"They were having an affair, Stanley."

"So he is saving her honor? He's willing to go to prison to do hard labor for thirty years, just to keep her name out of it?" He sipped his drink then shook his head. "But why is that a sacrifice? Why plead guilty when he could have just brazened it out in court. With a good lawyer he could even have gotten away with it."

"I think it was a sacrifice, because Carlton was playing chess. Or rather, Esme Levine was playing chess with him. The other night Carlton told me that she was actually a better chess player than him. And if you think back, Stanley, you will remember that when she asked him why he had been poisoning her, she then asked who else could have done. That was a clue I should have picked up on. She was telling him that unless he admitted it, she would draw Fiona Parker into it all. She knew that they were having an affair, you see."

Stanley drained his drink. "Wow! It is all possible, George, but unless Carlton was prepared to admit that he was having an affair, how is any of this relevant? How could it make matters any different?"

George leaned forward. "The missing cat may be the answer, Stanley. It liked cinnamon and arrowroot biscuits that Fiona Parker made for Esme. I think they were made with a recipe from a book she teaches from. *Mrs. Beeton's Book of Household Management*, that was it. I actually saw the cat licking one of the biscuits and going off with it. Then it disappeared a few days ago. It may have died from arsenic poisoning, not gone missing."

He shook his head. "So you see, it could be much worse than we believed. Suppose those biscuits that Fiona kept sending Esme via Carlton, which Esme may have become dependent on, were made with arsenic in them."

"Good grief! I see what you mean. You mean that Fiona Parker might have been the poisoner? But why should you think that?"

"I'm only speculating here, but she is a widow. She lost her husband to suspected gastro-enteritis during an epidemic a couple of years ago. Stanley, it is possible he died from arsenic poisoning. The symptoms of acute arsenic poisoning are exactly like gastro-enteritis."

"Good Lord, George. We've got to tell Sheriff Kelton."

George stared at his cold pipe. "There is another possibility, though." He leaned closer and signaled for Stanley to do the same. "I am worried that—"

Suddenly, someone banged a bottle on the bar to attract everyone's attention. They looked around to see an inebriated miner jump up on the counter.

"It's a disgrace, that's what it is," he cried. "I know it, you know it and the whole town knows it. We've got us a man who tried to poison his wife over in the jail and he's going to just walk away from what he deserves."

"What does he deserve?" someone yelled.

"The rope!"

Murmurs of assent spread around the saloon

George looked worriedly at Stanley. "I thought this might happen."

"What can we do, George? The mood of this crowd looks ugly and half of them are drunk already."

"We've got to think and act fast, that's what.

You slip out and go tell the sheriff what is brewing, but don't mention what we've just been talking about. If the same thing is happening in other saloons, then God help us. Carlton Levine is in grave danger of being lynched."

"What are you going to do, George?"

"I'm going to get hold of Judge Robinson."

They both left, unaware that someone in the crowd had been listening intently to them. They were also unaware that the eavesdropper was only a few paces behind as they emerged into the darkness.

# Chapter 12
## HELL'S DOOR

Carlton Levine was lying on the bunk in his cell when he became aware of the noise outside. It seemed to be more raucous than usual, as if some sort of Saturday night celebrations had stirred the town up. But then he heard a gunshot and the murmur of angry voices from a few streets away.

A footstep in the corridor between the sheriff's office and the cells caused him to sit up.

"What's going on?" he asked Deputy Bill Meade, a tall man in his late twenties.

"I don't know, but I'm going to find out. Sheriff Kelton told me to let you know that he's in the office himself and that you can have coffee when I get back."

Carlton did not feel reassured by the news. Especially not when he had heard a gunshot.

George had gone across the street and started down an alley when he heard the explosion of a gunshot behind him. Then he heard a zing and felt a shooting pain on his cheek and a simultaneous fierce thump in his back that threw him forwards. He struggled to stay on his feet.

After all of the bullets he had dug out of men

he had wondered what being shot would feel like. And now that he had, part of his mind immediately started analyzing what organs would be injured by a bullet hitting him in the right side of his back below the ribs. And there would not be anyone with his surgical skills to work on him.

His knees started to buckle and his hand went automatically to his back where he had been struck. In that moment he realized that there was no blood there. It felt dry, unlike the moistness on his right cheek, which he knew must be bleeding.

He could analyze it no further than that, for in that moment he heard a strange whistling cry and heard heavy footsteps racing at him from behind. To finish him off, he had no doubt.

"I'll get you this time, you damned doctor from hell!"

George's old boxing instincts rose to the surface. He forced his legs to hold up and he dodged to the left as he wheeled around, coming up with his fists ready.

The huge miner Red Douglas had swiped downwards with the old pistol that he had fired at George. The dodge had saved him, but George was well aware that the pistol could still do him great damage if he allowed Douglas to connect with him.

His head cleared and he ignored the pain in his back. He moved in and delivered two swift jabs to the miner's chin. They caused Douglas's head to snap back momentarily. Then with a whistling cry of rage he threw the pistol aside and launched himself at George with both fists flailing.

Anger in a boxing opponent was always a good sign, George knew. He never allowed himself to lose his temper in a fight, for once you did, you no longer had control over your actions. He was able to easily parry and block the miner's blows, then went in with a jab to the chin and then by a straight right to the throat, aiming precisely at the tracheotomy hole.

Red Douglas winced and clutched his hands to his throat. He groaned in pain.

George followed up with another straight right to the stomach and then with a left uppercut to the chin.

The miner flew backwards to land in a crumpled heap.

George picked up the discarded pistol and threw it away.

"What's going on here?" a voice called from the alley entrance.

George recognized it as belonging to Lance Brady, one of the town's deputy marshals.

"This man is called Red Douglas. He just tried to shoot me," George replied. "I'd appreciate it if you'd handcuff him and throw him in a cell."

As the deputy obliged George pulled off his jacket and held it up to the moonlight. A bullet hole was visible.

He turned his back to the deputy. "Is there a wound in my back, Deputy?"

Lance Brady's face registered surprise. "What are you made of, Doc. Iron? He reached up and pulled a metal slug from an indent in George's back.

"It's hot, but it didn't go any further. Darnedest thing I ever saw."

George was aware of the pain again, an area the size of a fist, as if he had been thumped by an iron glove worn by Red Douglas.

"Give me that, would you. I need to look at it later."

Then it occurred to him that the zinging noise had been from a bullet ricocheting of the brick wall of a building before it had struck him in the back. A gouged out brick fragment must have scored his cheek.

He deposited the slug in his pocket and replaced his jacket. "I can't stop, I have to get somewhere. Do me a favor and don't let this guy out until I get to see him."

"You'll be pressing charges, Doc?"

"You bet I will. But I'll also want to make sure the big bear pays me for saving his life last time."

Lance stood up. "I'd better see what all this noise is about, once I've locked him up," he said. "It doesn't sound healthy."

"I think you are right there. And you know

what mobs can do. I'd suggest that after you take care of him you get down to the County Sheriff's office. There could be big trouble ahead."

About half an hour later Sheriff C.B. Kelton and Deputy Bill Meade had stationed themselves on the steps outside the Cochise County Courthouse in readiness as the crowd noisily made its way down Third Street from Allen Street. There were several men at the front carrying lit torches and many firearms were in evidence.

"That's far enough!" Sheriff Kelton called. "Whatever you men think you are about to do, you can think again."

"We're bringing justice to a poor woman!" someone cried.

"There's a murdering dog in that jail you're protecting. He doesn't deserve to live."

"He needs hanging."

Sheriff Kelton raised his shotgun. "There will be no lynching in Tombstone! Now all of you, disperse before some of you get hurt."

"You can't take all of us, Sheriff."

"That gallows behind the courthouse is made for this purpose."

"I said get back! This is the last warning."

Suddenly, there was the loud clanging of a bell from further along Toughnut Street.

"Hold up, all of you!" cried out George Goodfellow. "Carlton Levine is innocent."

Everyone looked around to see that the town doctor was coming towards them, vigorously shaking the Tombstone School handbell. He was not alone. Judge James Robinson and Fiona Parker were walking on either side of him.

"What Doctor Goodfellow just said is true!" the judge cried out. "I have satisfied myself that this is the case and I have here a legal document calling for his immediate release."

"Are you serious, judge?" one of the ringleaders asked.

"I am deadly serious and it is official. Now all of you, do as the sheriff says, disperse and go to your homes."

There was much muttering and exclamations of astonishment and not a few of disappointment, but gradually the crowd turned and filtered away, to their homes or back to the various saloons.

Stanley Bagg came out of the courthouse, a spare shotgun cradled in his arms. He saw Fiona Parker with George and the judge.

"What's going on, George?" he asked in amazement.

"Exactly what I was about to ask," said the sheriff.

"We need to free Carlton and let Fiona here see him. I think they'll both be pleased to see each other. But first, I have to give him some bad news."

• • •

Carlton Levine was shocked to receive George's news that his wife was dead.

He sat in Sheriff Kelton's office, beside Fiona Parker. They were holding hands and staring at him as he recounted all that had happened. The sheriff, Stanley and the judge were also eager to have everything explained to them.

"Stanley and I worked out that you had sacrificed yourself, Carlton," he said.

Carlton sighed. "I am hurting so much inside, right now." He shook his head. "I don't think anyone in Tombstone ever realized just what a vindictive woman my wife Esme was. I had tried to make her happy, but when I fell in love with Fiona, I think she determined to make me suffer."

"That is how it seems, Carlton," George agreed. "She had been slowly poisoning herself with arsenic for some weeks. And now, when she thought that she had achieved her aim, she took a final fatal dose. Judge Robinson and I found her dead in her bed this evening."

Carlton squeezed Fiona's hand. "When Doctor Goodfellow found arsenic in her system he naturally assumed that I had been trying to poison her," he explained to her. "Then when the sheriff was there she implied to me that she was prepared to say that you had a hand in it, too, Fiona."

"That is exactly the case," George went on. "She had planned it all thoroughly, even to the point of including me in her web. She painstakingly made me aware that Fiona regularly sent her cinnamon and arrowroot biscuits, with a sprinkling of cinnamon on them. She fed them to Tabitha her cat in front of me. Then at some stage I believe she killed and probably buried the cat, so that if necessary she could imply that the poison was delivered to her in those biscuits."

"Which is what you at first suspected, George," Stanley said, as he lit one of his cigars.

"But then I also considered that there might be an alternative explanation. I was about to tell you, just before things flared up in the saloon. She had let me know that she knew about the liaison between you two."

He explained his theory about chess, just as he had done to Stanley earlier in the saloon.

"If I was right in my supposition that she was playing chess with you, Carlton, then she had accepted your sacrifice. And if she had accepted that sacrifice, then that meant that she had another move to make if she needed to. That meant that she knew that you hadn't poisoned her and it suggested to me that she knew who it was. Logically, it meant that it couldn't be Fiona, because if she merely suspected that, she could eliminate her rival at one swift swoop. It left me with the conclusion that she knew it wasn't Fiona, because she was actually poisoning herself."

"This is all incredible," said the sheriff.

"But it is true, I am afraid," added the judge. "I don't feel good about this, myself, since I had sentenced Mister Levine to a life of misery. When Doctor Goodfellow came to my house and told me of his suspicions I went with him to the house. And that is where we found her, dead by her own hand."

Carlton gasped and Fiona squeezed his hand. "I am so sorry, Carlton, my love."

The judge removed a letter from his pocket. "I have kept this letter that she wrote to Doctor Goodfellow for my report. She knew that she was going to kill herself, so she was satisfied that she had achieved her aim. Doctor Goodfellow and I are of the same opinion that she probably wrote it this evening when she thought that a lynch mob would hang Mister Levine. Then as soon as she had written it, she took her final, fatal dose of poison." He handed the letter to George. "Would you care to explain?"

George opened the envelope and took out the letter. "I think if I just read it to you, it explains everything:

"Dear Doctor Goodfellow,
As you read this I expect that both I and my husband will be dead.
I apologize to you, most sincerely, for refusing your offers to operate on me, and to admit me to hospital. Neither was part

of my plan, for you see, my life has been so miserable that I had decided to take my life.

I have known for some years that I have tumors on my womb. My last doctor diagnosed them as fibroids. He said that they would not harm me, but they would make it likely that I would never have children. That was the bitterest blow in my life.

My husband, as you now know, is in love with a trollop. I am sorry to have fooled you into thinking that I was ill with a malignancy, when it was actually from the small daily doses of arsenic I have been taking. In case you are interested, I obtained it from a supply of rat poison that we keep in the kitchen.

My husband believes that I planned to implicate his trollop. That is not necessary. I believe that the good people of Tombstone are about to end his miserable life very soon. And the misery that this causes her will be my gift to her for stealing him from me.

Yours most sincerely,
Esme Levine."

He replaced the letter in the envelope and handed it back to Judge Robinson.

Fiona began to weep and Carlton comforted her.

"We will leave Tombstone, my love," he said as he tried to comfort her.

"I have to say, I don't know how to report this in the *Epitaph*," Stanley said, as he stubbed out his cigar in an ashtray.

"There will have to be an official hearing," Judge Robinson said. "Can I suggest that you hold back until then, considering the sensitivity of this matter?"

Later that evening, when George got home and explained everything to Stella as well as giving Edith a watered down version, he examined his back in the mirror in his bedroom. A large purple bruise had started to form over his back below the ribs. He looked at the multiple layers of silk that he had fashioned into a vest and that he had taken to wearing under his shirt.

A good thing that Red Douglas hadn't used too much powder or it could have ended very differently for me tonight, he mused to himself. And a really good thing that he missed and I was only hit by a ricochet. If he had killed me then Carlton would probably have been hanged and the letter to him might never have been opened.

He made a mental note to himself to write a paper about his bulletproof vest.

He yawned. He suddenly felt tired. Very tired.

• • •

In October George received a formal invitation to join the Southern Pacific Railroad as their physician. It would mean a substantial amount of money and a move to Tucson.

He announced it to Stella and Edith over breakfast.

"Are we going to go, Daddy?" Edith asked.

"I think so, Princess. I have just about done all that I can here in Tombstone. I believe it is time to move on to new pastures."

"You will be badly missed in Tombstone," Stella said. "People like Camillus Fly and Stanley Bagg will find life very dull without you."

"Oh, I don't know, I think life will always be exciting in a place like Tombstone. It's a town that is just too tough to die."

But although he didn't tell them, his recent experience of being shot in the back, and only being saved by his bulletproof vest, had been instrumental in making his decision. He had no desire to end up in Tombstone's Boothill Graveyard.

It was time to go.

# Author's Note

This is a work of fiction based around events in the life of the very real Doctor George Emory Goodfellow (1855-1910), often known as the Surgeon to the Gunfighters. It is set in Tombstone, Arizona, where he practiced as a physician and surgeon from 1880 to 1891. During his years there, in "the town too tough to die," he rubbed shoulders with such characters of the Wild West as Wyatt Earp and his brothers Morgan and Virgil, Doc Holiday, Bat Masterton and Luke Short. He actually did treat the victims of the Gunfight at the O.K. Corral. And he regretted that he was unable to save his friend Dr. John Handy, as mentioned in this novel.

He was a truly pioneering surgeon. Throughout his career he established a reputation as the foremost expert on gunshot wounds, as well as being the first surgeon to perform a perineal prostatectomy along with other "first" operations.

He wrote and published many medical papers in the journals of the day. His work on the impenetrability of silk would lead to the actual bulletproof vests of the future.

He was also a scientist, an expert in mining and geology. His research into Gila Monsters was published in The Scientific American. And in his youth he had been the boxing champion at the United States Naval Academy at Annapolis.

There is a wealth of information written about his larger than life character. The excellent biography, *Dr. Goodfellow—Physician to the Gunfighters, Scholar, and Bon Vivant* by Don Chaput, published by Westernlore Press will give a good overview.

# About the Author

Clay More is the western pen-name of Keith Souter, a part time doctor, medical journalist and novelist. He lives and works within arrowshot of the ruins of a medieval castle in England. In 2014 he was elected as Vice President of Western Fictioneers and he is also a member of Western Writers of America, The Crime Writers' Association, International Thriller Writers and several other writers organizations.

He writes novels in four genres—crime as Keith Moray, Westerns as Clay More, Historical crime and YA as Keith Souter. His medical background finds its way into a lot of his writing, as can be seen in this novel about Doctor George Goodfellow as well as in most of his western novels and short stories. His character in *Wolf Creek* is Doctor Logan Munro, the town doctor, who is gradually revealing more about himself with each book he appears in. Another of his characters is Doctor Marcus Quigley, dentist, gambler and bounty hunter. He has recently published a collection of short stories about him in *Adventures from the Casebook of D Marcus Quigley*, published by High Noon Press.

If you care to find out more about him visit his website: http://www.keithsouter.co.uk

Or his blog http://moreontherange.blogspot.co.uk

Or check out his regular contribution about 19th Century Medicine on the WF blog http://westernfictioneers.blogspot.com.

Books are produced in the United States using U.S.-based materials

Books are printed using a revolutionary new process called THINKtech™ that lowers energy usage by 70% and increases overall quality

Books are durable and flexible because of Smyth-sewing

Paper is sourced using environmentally responsible foresting methods and the paper is acid-free

**Center Point Large Print**
600 Brooks Road / PO Box 1
Thorndike, ME 04986-0001 USA

(207) 568-3717

**US & Canada:**
1 800 929-9108
www.centerpointlargeprint.com